NAYANTARA SAHGAL is the author of several works of fiction and non-fiction, the first of which, *Prison and Chocolate Cake*, an autobiography, was published in 1954. Her works include classic novels such as *Rich Like Us*, *Plans for Departure* and *Lesser Breeds*. She has received the Sahitya Akademi Award, the Sinclair Prize and the Commonwealth Writers' Prize. She is a Member of the American Academy of Arts & Sciences. She has been awarded the Diploma of Honour from the International Order of Volunteers of Peace (Italy), and an Honorary Doctorate of Letters from the University of Leeds. She returned her Akademi Award in 2015 in protest against the murder by vigilantes of three writers,and the Akademi's silence at the time.She has been a Vice President of the PUCL (People's Union for Civil Liberties) andis engaged in an ongoing protest againstthe assaults on the freedom of expression and democratic rights.

Fiction

A Time to be Happy (1958)

This Time of Morning (1962)

Storm in Chandigarh (1969)

The Day in Shadow (1971-72)

A Situation in New Delhi (1977)

Rich Like Us (1985)

Plans For Departure (1986)

Mistaken Identity (1988)

Lesser Breeds (2003)

Day of Reckoning (*Short Stories*) (2015)

Non-Fiction

Prison and Chocolate Cake (1954)

From Fear Set Free (1962)

Point of View (1997)

Before Freedom: Nehru's Letters to His Sister 1909-1947
(Edited and with an Introduction) (2000)

Relationship (with E.N.Mangat Rai) (2008)

Jawaharlal Nehru: Civilizing a Savage World (2010)

Indira Gandhi: Tryst With Power (2012)

The Story of India's Freedom Movement (2013)

The Political Imagination (2014)

Nehru's India: Essays on the Maker of a Nation
(Edited and with an Introduction) (2015)

When the
Moon Shines
by Day

NAYANTARA SAHGAL

SPEAKING
TIGER

SPEAKING TIGER PUBLISHING PVT. LTD
4381/4, Ansari Road, Daryaganj
New Delhi 110002

Copyright © Nayantara Sahgal 2017

First published in India by Speaking Tiger 2017

ISBN: 978-93-86702-14-2
eISBN: 978-93-86702-13-5

10 9 8 7 6 5 4 3 2 1

The moral right of the author has been asserted.

Typeset in Adobe Garamond Pro by SÜRYA, New Delhi
Printed at Sanat Printers, Kundli

For Kiran Nagarkar,
a great storyteller,
this story of our times

The woman was at an angle that made a slanting question mark of her figure—a tilt at which it was impossible to stand, much less take a step forward, which was what the tip of one foot was doing. Her garment fell curving from shoulder to hip, flared out behind her knee and swirled round to her ankle. The thick-looking stuff of it could not possibly have that fluid flow and flare, yet it did. Her figure was in profile, but her face turned outward showing slits for eyes and mouth under a head of elaborately arranged hair pierced by the long straight ornamental sticks that adorn Japanese headdresses.

The scroll hung on her bedroom wall where she could see it first thing in the morning when she opened her eyes. Its contradictions made mysterious artistic sense. The weighty cloth dipped and flowed airily. The figure's moving foot stood still. All of which connected it with the Japanese author's book she had chosen for discussion at the book get-together today.

'He's a British national, Rehana, so you can't call him a Japanese author, and we had a British book last time,' Nandini had objected.

True enough, but the novel had been a favourite of Rehana's since she had read it years ago when it first came out. No setting could be more English—the Lord and Lady, inherited acres, the manor with its vast retinue of maids, footmen, butler. Aristocracy and hierarchy in its heyday in an atmosphere of forever more. Britain in the 1930s. Then who would have expected such a noiseless Japanese way of unravelling such an English story? It was the way the two melled— like Yehudi Menuhin's violin and Ravi Shankar's sitar making music together—that made the book a magical read. You could hear a pin drop in the Japanese stillness of the storytelling, however English the story.

The book club had been Nandini's idea. She had her doubts about discussing such an old novel when they could hardly keep up with all the new books coming out. Rehana had persuaded her to count it as new since it was a new revised edition. It had a special fascination for her, having grown up with her father's memories of the 1930s when he was a student in London. Peacetime though it was, the Hitler-Mussolini arsenal of terrifying newly minted armaments was pounding Spain's towns and Spanish lives to rubble in support of the generalissimo who had overthrown Spain's elected government. The two dictators had chosen the Iberian peninsula to try out their weapons for war-worthiness.

'Didn't any country help the Spanish republic?' she had asked her father.

Not a single country did, he had said, still angry years later about Europe's callous indifference. Europe's democracies sat by and watched. It's not our war, they said. For them it was dust, death and foreign furore far south. It was civil war on the outer edge of Europe in a country that was European by a hair's breadth. The mess down there was being taken care of by the Europeans who knew what to do about it. It was nothing to worry about as Generalissimo Franco was getting all the support he needed. So it was not surprising, Rehana recalled when she re-read the novel she had chosen, that war did not figure in conversation at the manor. For the manor life carried on as it always had and always would. English teas on green English lawns, breakfasts on a sideboard loaded with bacon, kidneys, kippers, kedgeree and left half uneaten, and five-course black-tie dinners to which the men who governed England came. The centipedal crawl of fascism slithering through the story was conspicuous by its absence from the manor's pleasant days and nights.

Papa had clarified that though no government had moved a muscle to help the beleaguered Spanish republic, thousands of volunteers from many countries had gone to fight for Spain. But courage, conviction and passion were up against the deadliest war machine the world had ever seen and they were easy prey for the armed fury let loose on Spain by Franco's friends.

His own personal memory of the time was of his seventeen-year-old self jammed in the crowd of thousands in Trafalgar Square at the meeting organized by the republic's supporters. From where he stood, straining to see above the higher heads in front of him, he saw the slim silhouette of an Indian in a black shervani and black Gandhi cap speaking from a platform below Nelson's statue. The speaker had one arm flung out making its passionate point. He was telling them he had just come back from Barcelona.

'There I entered this Europe of conflict. There I remained for five days and watched the bombs fall nightly from the air. There in the midst of want and destruction I felt more at peace with myself than anywhere else in Europe. There was light there, the light of courage and determination and of doing something worthwhile. Spain was not Spain only but a world locked in a death struggle with the barbarian hordes of reaction and brutal violence. Spain and Czechoslovakia represented to me precious values in life. If I deserted them, what would I cherish in India? For what kind of freedom do we struggle?'

Nehru's words had found a resounding echo in the crowd.

The rehearsal in Spain for the world war to come, said Papa, would have been wiped clear out of human memory if it hadn't been for the novels written about it; if the desperate screams of the dying and the terror engulfing the city of

Guernica had not survived in Picasso's painting of Guernica being pulverized one Monday afternoon in April 1937. What if only the destroyers' versions had survived? In one of these the Nazi commander of the aerial bombardment had noted triumphantly in his diary: 'Guernica, a city with five thousand residents, has been literally razed to the ground. Bomb craters can be seen in the streets. Simply wonderful.' In another, a Nazi general had recorded that combat experience in the field like this trial run was far more useful than ten years of military training in peacetime. And Generalissimo Franco's version let it be known it was retreating republicans who had destroyed the city.

That is why novels have to be written, Rehana, and paintings have to be painted, Papa had said. Without art and literature we would never know the truth.

He was a historian himself but he had a personal interest in works of art because his closest friend, Nikhil, was a well-known artist, and as time went on, one of the best.

~

Kamlesh was looking forward to lunch. It was three years since he and Franz Rohner had met. They had had Fellowships at the Lyleford Institute in New York and had foregathered with other Fellows in the central hall for convivial get-togethers over vintage sherries at midday—a welcome break from a morning's concentration. Sometimes he and Franz had carried on talking over lunch in the institute's dining room. Franz was lively company and his subject was revolutions—French, Russian, Italian, German, and other historic convulsions of the Left or Right. What had made his books popular reading was his entertaining approach. He could describe a horrifying event in excruciating detail in language that made an absurdity of it. Kamlesh had seen that done brilliantly on film. Chaplin's Hitler had been reduced to idiotic antics in *The Great Dictator*, but no one had done quite this in writing. He couldn't remember which revolution Franz had been working on at the institute, but that project had now been published and he was in India for the launch of its Indian edition.

Kamlesh went through security at the entrance and walked into the lobby of the Ashwin, the newly opened hotel where Franz's publisher had put him up. The publisher was doing him proud. Five-star was the norm; the Ashwin was a six-star. Obviously he was certain of record sales. It was his own first time in the hotel and he glanced around the immense high-ceilinged crystal-chandeliered lobby. Who invented chandeliers? It must take a high-wire trapeze act to clean them. The purpose of chandeliers in their heavenly abode might well be to show they are on high and you are below and make sure you know the difference. Soaring walls and glass-like expanses of floor gleamed golden-beige under concealed lighting. Other people had built Taj Mahals and the like. This must be a monument to the prosperity we didn't yet have. The fountain in the middle of the lobby had a low marble surround you could sit on and peer down into its marble base studded with clusters of what looked like rubies, emeralds and sapphires glinting and glimmering in a chandelier's underwater light. Several hotel guests standing beside him were admiring the jewelled effect. A child leaned over too far and was yanked back by a parental hand to keep her from toppling over. Her shriek startled Kamlesh out of his reverie. Hotel staff were moving around, guests were checking out, checking in. Suitcases were being wheeled in, baggage was being trundled out on trolleys. The lobby was as busy and bustling with activity as any hotel lobby. Bemused by its appearance of immense emptiness, he hadn't noticed. Strange what the arrangement of bricks and stone known as architecture could do.

The reception counter was brightly lit. The man behind it said 'Bharat Mata ki Jai' and Kamlesh asked for Franz's room number. He was told the gentleman was awaiting him in the dining room. Directed to the distant end of the lobby he stopped on the way to look into the bookshop and saw copies of Franz's book prominently displayed beside shiny hardcovers of *Mein Kampf*. The irony of the Nazi bible being displayed alongside Franz's book—Franz who was famous for satirizing the Fuhrer and his kind—made Kamlesh smile. The dining room was well filled but Kamlesh spotted Franz at once. There he was, at a window table, handsomely blond, sitting straight and tall in spite of his age. There had never been any scholarly slouch about him. He had not mentioned his wife would be with him but she was there beside him and Kamlesh was struck once again by their resemblance to each other. One could easily take them for brother and sister. They had the same grey-blond good looks, blue eyes and, at least in his own inexpert judgement, a Scandinavian more than a German fairness.

Greetings and handshakes were boisterous and Kamlesh sat down opposite Gerda. Catching up waited till they had ordered, and there was no ordering until the menu had been seriously perused, as had the menu in the Lyleford dining room. The maitre d' waved the waiter away, set menus before them himself and stood by for their order. Franz ruled out salad, causing Gerda to courteously explain, 'You see, we have been advised not to eat raw vegetables in India, and fruit only if we have peeled it ourselves.' The maitre d' assured them the fruit and vegetables were grown on Mr Ashwin's own farm and, raw or cooked, they were most safe. An array of crisp greens arrived while Franz and Gerda, their heads lowered and touching over the menu, conferred lengthily about the main course and decided on seafood. Someone had told Franz there was a fish restaurant not far from here that had lobsters flown fresh and live, not frozen, from the west coast. It made all the difference to the flavour. They brought these live creatures to your table in a clay pot of water for you to choose one before they took it away and plunged it into boiling water. Of course they couldn't bring clay pots around in this dining room but the maitre d' assured them that here, too, they got consignments of freshly caught lobster flown up from the coast and cooked alive on demand. Kamlesh remembered that Franz was as particular about what he ate as about his views on revolutions, and had the same flair for dissecting every aspect of both. His own order of filet of sole, easy to slice and eat, compared tamely with the ritual of hot melted butter drizzled onto lobster, succulent white flesh gouged out of its shell by the forkful and lifted again and again to waiting expectant mouths, while eyelids drooped in blissful acknowledgment of expectation fulfilled.

'So how are things going on here?' asked Franz between mouthfuls.

A vague general answer would not do. Kamlesh knew Franz's practical mind dealt in verifiable specifics. Seeing the maitre d' engaged elsewhere in the dining room, he tried to be specific about something as intangible as atmosphere, which was all he had to go by. Did atmosphere have a beginning? Was it the bullets that bloodied a prayer ground in January 1948? Or the prancing and capering years later on the wrecked and shattered dome of a mosque? Or after that when death danced through a city? Or long before any of that? When had it begun?

Kamlesh heard himself pondering possibilities but he must have sounded factual enough because in an abrupt change of mood Franz said sharply, 'Religion joined to nation is a marriage made in hell. We know this in Germany.'

Religion and Germany? What had religion to do with Germany? What was Franz talking about? But the maitre d' arrived to enquire if all was satisfactory. It was. Their plates were removed and an unpronounceable dessert was pointed out on the menu. All three of them agreed to it, and then Franz wanted to know what he was writing.

At the Lyleford Institute Kamlesh had been completing the book he had titled *Genie Out of the Bottle*. Hardly a suitable title for the Non-Aligned Movement, his publisher, Sudhir, had objected. But it was just right for the magician's act it had been, Kamlesh had argued, and quoted a poet who had got to the heart and soul of it. Richard Wright, black American, had written of the men who launched the Movement at Bandung: 'Only black, brown and yellow men could have felt the need for such a meeting. There was something extra-political, extra-social, almost extra-human about it. It smacked of tidal waves, of natural forces. The agenda and the subject matter had been written for centuries in the blood and bones of the participants.' Poets will be poets, Sudhir had shrugged, unimpressed, but what had poetry to do with politics? Kamlesh knew of moods and moments in history when it inexplicably had, and he had stuck to his title.

'Now that I'm posted back here,' he said, 'I'm working on the Taj Mahal story.'

'What is there to write about the Taj Mahal?' enquired Gerda. 'It is there to see and wonder at.'

Not only, Kamlesh told her. It had been remarked on by foreign travellers from far and wide. No Mughal building, maybe no building anywhere, had attracted so much interest. He was no architect himself. but was there anyone who remained unaffected by extraordinary architecture? Walk into the Duomo in Milan and be spellbound. Stand on a sidewalk in New York, look up at a skyscraper and feel your head spin. Let your eyes encircle the serene symmetry of a mosque.

'But what about the romance? I hope you will

not leave out the romance, the love story which is the reason for it.'

He assured her he would not, and asked Franz which revolution his new book was about.

'It is about several. It is a jumble. What does it matter which one? After all they are much the same.'

This was a subject they had argued about before, a losing battle for Kamlesh whose contention that they were poles apart in ideas and aims cut no ice with Franz.

'Once in power they are the same,' said Franz. 'Blood brothers could not be more alike. And whose atrocities are worse we do not know. This kaiserschmarn is excellent.'

'Delicious,' breathed Gerda, spooning more whipped cream on the scramble of pancake and apple sauce on her plate, 'and fancy finding a Bavarian dessert here.'

Going back to atrocities, Kamlesh observed that some had been worse than others.

'As we know,' Franz agreed, but added, 'The human race has been created cruel. How else to explain the family outings to watch hangings and beheadings, or the lusty cheers when the guillotine struck. But wait, let me think of a homemade example, an ordinary family custom…like your plain and simple widow-burning used to be.' And he came up with foot-binding. 'Note the scientific care with which it was done. First cutting the woman's toenails and soaking her feet in hot water to soften up the skin. Then massaging them with alum. After that breaking every toe except the big toe and folding them under the sole of the foot…'

'Please, Franz,' Gerda pleaded with an anguished intensity that went deeper than a protest against these gory details. It came to Kamlesh that Franz's recital chillingly lacked the saving grace of his trademark humour.

'Then the feet are tightly bound to break the arches. After this they are laid into shoes designed for feet that will never walk again. For a thousand years they will only hobble. And if you ask, is this not cruelty? they will be surprised. No, no, it is a household practice to keep her in her womanly place. Torture comes naturally to the human species and it begins at home. How scientifically it is planned, Kamlesh, to achieve the desired result—the tool to break the toes, the shoe for what the foot has become. My dear Kamlesh, in matters of cruelty I am beyond surprise.'

They finished their coffee in silence. The silence lengthened. A waiter brought marzipan candies. Kamlesh tried to think of something to say.

'What will you write next?' he finally asked.

Gerda's hands were lying limply on the table. Franz covered them with one of his own, as if in apology. He sounded more like himself when he spoke.

'I am thinking of writing about a family matter. Did we tell you we will not be returning directly to Europe after our time here? We are planning to take a cruise from Mumbai to wherever it takes us. Gerda will swim and lie in the sun. I will recollect and scribble. In the evenings we will drink and dance the nights away.'

Kamlesh took leave of them in the lobby, saying he would be there at the book launch the following evening.

~

Rehana never knew how to describe Nikhil's paintings. They had a physical strength one was not prepared for from paint laid on canvas. Dense, intense colour and all the shades of its absence gave his paintings a violence that spoke. You saw the filth-crusted plodding feet, the sweat and grime with new astonished eyes. So, too, the one-legged beggar girl hopping in the treacherous inches between two rows of cars. So, too, the grim grey interior of some confine where a naked woman lies. Her arms have been dragged up, manacled at the wrists and roped to something further up. Her mouth gapes in a scream you can hear being torn out of it by a paintbrush that makes remorseless use of dark and light.

A critic once asked Nikhil why he was so obsessed with dismal subjects and he had retorted that his obsession was with colour. Subjects were what happened to be there. Except of course the giant loaf of bread that filled the cloudless sky of one canvas. The loaf is mightily risen and the heavenly halo encircling it is blindingly luminous. On earth far below it a tiny man in a langot lies prostrate, face-down in slush. His ribs poke through his skin like you see in emaciated cattle. His mud-spattered arms grope forward straining to join his palms in prayer.

'What is this celestial loaf supposed to mean?' Papa had demanded.

'It means what you see: "For the poor man God is a loaf of bread". Except that Gandhi got it wrong. This poor wretch shouldn't be worshipping a "double roti" he's never heard of. He should be praying to a chappati.' Nikhil laughed his infectious irresistible laugh.

The sound of his laughter filled food-and-drink evenings at home. He and her parents spoke the tri-language that was natural to them, starting in one language, slipping into another if it was better suited to what they were describing. Rehana had grown up believing their interwoven Hindi-Urdu-English was one and the same entrancing language. They had named her Rehana because they liked the sound of it. Like their language, their world had no frontiers either. What they knew of Europe they had made their own. Nikhil said Prague was Europe's most beautiful city, Mama said Budapest. Whichever was, they agreed Europe's most beautiful people were born of Europe's collision with Asia. The magic was in the mix.

The heartbreaking news coming over the radio from a Europe being devastated by war had moved them to tears and had taught Rehana that when such things happen the heart has no boundaries. She heard them recall the speaker at Trafalgar Square who had made the Nazi war on Spain and the invasion of Czechoslovakia his own grim personal concern. 'Spain and Czechoslovakia represented to me precious values in life,' he had said, 'If I deserted them, what would I cherish in India? For what kind of freedom do we struggle?' For them his impassioned avowal became a call to arms of another kind, drawing them into Gandhi's weaponless fight for freedom from British rule.

Nikhil had served one long sentence, her parents two each for the treason of refusing allegiance to the King Emperor. What had it felt like hearing the massive iron jail gate clang shut behind you, having your watch, pen, wallet confiscated, even your handkerchief lest it be hiding subversion, and being marched to a barrack where another iron gate clanged shut, locking you and years of your life behind stone walls? Rehana marvelled at the ruggedness of their idealism and the times that had made it possible. The distance between then and now wasn't all that long but suddenly the present had no past. Papa's books on medieval India were gone from shop shelves, struck off curriculums and dropped from his publisher's list. Kamlesh had helped her to trace and collect as many as they could locate and she had stored them in two old leather suitcases that would take their weight.

Occupied with their work and the fullness of their lives after freedom, her parents had not harked back to their jailed years. When freedom came, song, dance, paint, poetry and much else cast off the shackles of what had gone before. An example had been set by the war that had broken free of war's violent history when Gandhi replaced it with civil disobedience and made non-violence the command that sent men and women into battle unarmed, something new under the sun.

The atmosphere of newness was electric. No one was harking back. Rehana would never have known what her parents had gone through during the years of struggle if it hadn't been for the diary Mama had kept of her last imprisonment. The only mention she had ever made of it was that she had been one of a hundred thousand prisoners and what had kept her going was the knowledge of that unknown unseen comradeship. Rehana still re-read bits of the diary from time to time though it was no less hurtful each time:

13 August 1942: I was conducted to the old familiar barrack. I had been away from this barrack for a year and a half and returning to it seemed a continuation of my second term in prison. It was 3:15 am. I spread my bedding on the ground, was locked in, and my second term of prison life began. My head ached badly and the throbbing in my temples prevented sleep. There is no water, no sanitary arrangements, nothing at all. In the morning

I got a little water from the convicts' bathing tap and washed my face. Towards noon some raw rations arrived but no coal, so cooking was not possible. Later with a convict's help I tried to make a small fire of twigs but the fire would not light. It is now six, lock-up time. The matron enquires what I will be having for dinner. I said what could I eat when there was nothing to eat. So ends the first day of my second term of imprisonment.

14 August 1942: Some raw rations have arrived on my second day, some vegetables and a bundle of firewood. The rations are mildewed and are mixed with grit and dirt, tiny stones and even a spider, maybe to make up the weight of what we are allowed. I cook it and I am so hungry that I eat it. So far there are no rats but they will come. Last time a family of rats had the run of the place.

Every now and again shouts of 'Inquilab Zindabad' and other slogans come to me from the men's barrack over the wall. I feel less lonely after that and, in a way, happier. Comfort, happiness, freedom, how meaningless these words have become.

16 August 1942: A woman who is in for murder told me she killed her husband because he thrashed her and starved her. The six-week-old baby girl she brought to jail with her died, and she had to leave her two-year-old son behind. She has not seen him since then. He is now eleven and she cries for him.

18 August 1942: There is a new rule for political prisoners. We will not be permitted newspapers, letters, interviews or any article from home. Jail clothes will be provided. Our allowance will be reduced from twelve annas to nine annas per day.

19 August 1942: This barrack is rectangular and made to accommodate twelve or more convicts. There are gratings along each side. The ceiling falls in chunks and makes a mess on the cot and on the floor. The door is bolted and locked every night. One side of the barrack is raised four steps from the ground and serves as a latrine after lock-up. I keep my jail cot at the furthest end of the barrack from the latrine. We are surrounded by high walls which shut out even the trees.

There is a door between my yard and the adjoining yard. The cells there are unfit for any human being. There is a woman there now who I can hear wailing through the day and the night. It is a horrible sound, the wail of a prisoner who has lost all hope and is afraid. Hearing it I haven't been able to sleep. When I finally did I dreamt I was in a solitary cell. It was hardly high enough for me to stand up in and by stretching my arms sideways I could touch the walls on either side. I cried to get out but the cell was locked and there was no escape. After this dream I couldn't sleep. A rhyme read long ago came to my mind:

As he went through cold Bath fields
he saw a solitary cell
And the Devil was pleased, for it gave
him a hint
For improving the prisons in Hell.

22 August 1942: The days are incredibly long and prison nights surely contain more hours than any others. In the evenings I like to sit near my grating and watch the drifting clouds pass in the sky and wait for the stars to come out. So far there is no moon but I wait for her to send a silver beam into my barrack by way of greeting and to show that she remembers me.

Abdul, her servant, interrupted her reading. She could never remember to call him Morari Lal, the name he had given to shopkeepers and street vendors in the bazaar. With the alertness essential for survival, he had heard before she did that Mussalmans were now regarded as outsiders who must wear a badge and live in a far-off settlement too far from his work here. So it was better to be Morari Lal in the street. Abdul was eighteen and had come a year ago from Jharkhand. It was not hard to imagine how he must have travelled. Rehana could see him in the train, crushed between bodies on a bench packed with bodies. He is welded to the bench. In his waking sleep his head jerks up and down and lurches sideways, hitting his neighbour's as the train rocks and jolts on its westward track. This punishment is called travel and there is no knowing what lies at the end of it. Station stops ease the numbness in his arms and legs and give him six minutes to swallow hot sweet tea and buy the food his coins allow. He chews it in cautious mouthfuls, making it last. There has never been enough of it to eat ravenously or he would have grown to his full height. If migrants migrate it must be because they must. Here the migrant network directs him to jobs and so to her house. He helps Gangu in the kitchen and does all the housework. He hasn't taken a holiday to go home. When she asked him why, he said in his rapid-fire way: mother-father dead in firing when village land seized by mining company, grandmother useless with weeping, sisters already given in marriage, uncle put him on train, giving her to understand there is no home to go back to.

Rehana had shown him how to work the washing machine. Minutes later he was still squatted in front of it watching blouses and brassieres, petticoats, towels, sheets and pillowcases being hurled around, which she had never thought of as an enthralling sight.

'Bibi,' Abdul told her, not for the first time, 'basement is damp. Abba-jan sahib's books should not be there.'

But where else could she store them, save them? Abdul emptied the suitcases every few days and spread the books out in the sun to save them from mildew and she dreamed of a dignified setting for Papa's life's work, a library where his books would be catalogued, numbered, taken out and kept in circulation.

The book discussion this afternoon at Nandini's was argumentative, as it often was. The four of them were in their late forties, all but herself with grown sons and daughters now on their own, studying or starting work. Nandini was the only one who was maternally inclined by nature but even she had not been interested in ruling the world via rocking the cradle as the saying went and had made a fabled success of running the confectionary side of her husband's catering business. Rehana's three close friends made the most of their well-earned release from parenting and all four enjoyed this time-out from the demands of their working lives. But books were more than a casual reason for getting together. They shared a curiosity about the art of story-making, the many and mysterious effects of words on a page that made for the spell-casting joy of literature. It was a time-out Rehana particularly valued because she thought of the three of them as belonging to normal life, and herself not quite, but basking in it through them. Unlike though they were, what they also had in common, or so it seemed to her, was the composure that comes of not having been trained to self-efface, and the book choices they made were interestingly different.

Rehana pointed out her chosen novel's sinister undercurrent which strangely had gone unnoticed in the manor. For the others this aspect of the story, so central to it, didn't ring true. How could the manor not have seen war was coming, especially when the men who governed the country came to dinner? Could they have sat at the dinner table downing vintage port and gone on about grouse-shoots, and their wives in another room about their daughters' debuts in society? Would the manor and its guests not have noticed they were about to be overrun by the tanks rolling over Europe? So, psychologically, it didn't add up. Tea ended with Aruna concluding that not realizing what was so plainly going on all around you couldn't happen in real life, but then of course this was fiction.

Rehana got home and remembered she had promised Kamlesh she would go with him to a book launch he had been invited to and he was coming to pick her up. He and Vineet had been friends and colleagues in the foreign service and he kept in affectionate touch.

~

Kamlesh, by virtue of being the Rohners' friend, and Rehana with him, were given front row seats next to Gerda and Mrs Ashwin, and were warmly greeted. Nalin Ashwin got up from his seat to welcome them. He was not at all what his multi-millions and the size and grandeur of his hotel, or his closeness to the highest in the land, had led Kamlesh to expect. Of medium height, his informal manner was charming and disarming. He told them he had taken a degree in political science at Princeton before going on to management and all that, hence his interest in the author whose work he greatly admired. The auditorium, not the hotel's largest but the one for cultural events, was soon full. Kamlesh guessed these were people who may not have read Franz, but had certainly heard about him, and had come to be entertained. Franz didn't disappoint them. He read a witty extract from his new book that set a light-hearted mood for the evening.

'Welcome to India, Mr Rohner,' smiled Nalin Ashwin in the conversation that followed, 'you are here at the best possible time. I won't call it a revolution, knowing your own suspicion of the word'—a nod of cheerful acknowledgement from Franz Rohner—'but a great cultural transformation. May I say we have learned a lot from the revival and rebirth of Germany between the wars—especially your pride in your Germanness. If sitting here on this stage you could look back and refashion the phenomenal rise of Germany, would you have kept its power at home and not advanced it across Europe— after reclaiming Austria and Czechoslovakia, of course, because those countries were part-German anyway.'

Franz heartily agreed that occupying Austria, Belgium, Holland, Czechoslovakia, Luxemburg, Poland, Norway, Denmark, Greece and Yugoslavia had not been a good idea. And the Czechs and Austrians too, had most certainly not enjoyed being occupied, part-German or part anything else that they might have been. We are all part something else, are we not? Who is purely one thing? And as for going too far, that is the trouble with revolutions.

Franz's turn of phrase and the string of occupied countries he ticked off on the raised fingers of both hands brought a collective chuckle from the audience.

'The other trouble with revolutions is, they are so boring. There was a novel in Stalin's time called *Cement*. You have guessed it, it was about cement. And then all the repetition. We had our Heil Hitlering. Spain went one better with ' Viva Generalissimo Franco Franco Franco'—yes, three Francos at a time. They all had the same stiff-armed salute'—Franz stood up and shot out his arm to demonstrate it—'but the Italians went one better. The hailing and heiling was not enough for them. As we know, they have music in their souls so they also hailed their Duce and 'fascismo' with song.'

To the audience's delight he sang it:

'Giovinezza, giovinezza
Primavera di belleza
Nel fascismo e la salvezza
Della nostra liberta
Per Benito Mussolini
Eia eia alala!'

The applause was enthusiastic and prolonged. Nalin joined in it. When it subsided he said, 'But, Mr Rohner, the truth is that many at that time looked to Italy and Germany for inspiration. It was Mussolini who advised our leader B.S. Moonje to give our youth sound military training when Moonje had an audience with him in the Palazzo Venzia in 1934. From the age of six a child's mind must be made ready for war, he said. Peace had to be based on millions of steel bayonets. Those were his very words. Moonje took them to heart and when he came home he set up the recruiting and training of children and youths for an armed militia like Mussolini's Balillas. To give them their due, can we deny that the two dictators, yours and the Italian, were greatly admired at one time?'

'Indeed they were,' agreed Franz, 'So was the crinoline. This was a hoop of a garment made of wire that swung out like a circular cage around the woman. Over it went a skirt and under it were petticoats upon petticoats made of horse's hair to hold the cage in place. When she sat down the hoop flew up so she must lower herself with caution. After the crinoline came the bustle. This was a lump of padding on her behind under her skirt to make her derriere stick out like a table in a posture that pushed her breast out in front. Breast out front, rump out behind. And both these were high fashion. They, too, were greatly admired—at one time.'

There was a lone cackle, then an extended roar of laughter from his listeners before the conversation could resume.

'Your books have parodied revolutions and you make them sound alike. But are they?' asked Nalin.

'Are they not?' Franz spread his hands wide. 'It has all happened before and it keeps happening, always as before. It is tiresome how they copycat each other, even to their craze for uniforms to carry out their commands. Black Shirts, Brown

Shirts. This is why a wise observer of that time wrote: "Three cheers for dear old Gandhi, Who wears no shirt at all!'"

The unfamiliar limerick caused more mirth.

Nalin persisted goodnaturedly, enjoying his task, 'We know from your books it's the violence you object to, but all through history it has been understood that the end justifies the means. As everyone knows, you can't make an omelette without breaking eggs.'

'Indeed you cannot, so why make an omelette? Is it not time to boil the eggs instead?'

More hilarity in which Nalin joined. When it died down he went on, 'Since you say they are all the same, how would you describe revolutions in a nutshell?'

Franz pondered this. 'In a nutshell, let me see. One and all, they come from the top,' he began. 'So in a nutshell, are they not the man who mounts his woman with no please-may-I, gallops to glory, rolls off his mount and snores himself to sleep? And the woman? Ah, the woman! She lies awake plotting how to kill him.'

After a second's shock, shouts of laughter erupted. When Nalin could make himself heard he said he assumed the woman is 'the people'. But didn't the people benefit at all from revolution? Oh yes, some few did, Franz conceded, oh yes, beyond their wildest dreams.

The quantity of books laid out were signed and sold and orders placed for more. At cocktails afterwards, Gerda told Arati Ashwin what a surprise it had been finding a Bavarian dessert on the menu and Arati said she collected national desserts when she travelled abroad with her husband. It was a hobby of hers and her dessert cookbook had done very well. Before leaving she told Gerda there would be a car at the Rohners' disposal for their shopping and sightseeing all the days they were here.

Rehana picked a morsel of camembert toothpicked to a wafer off the tray being offered, and another before the tray moved on. The man beside her took a couple too.

'These are very good,' he said, and like people at cocktail parties who don't know each other and will never meet again, they chatted pleasantly about nothing in particular.

Rehana was glad she had agreed to come with Kamlesh. She had been feeling bleak and miserable since Papa's books had been disappeared. Being among people in anonymous undemanding company helped. The author's well-known humour had had the curious effect of drawing her attention to what lay unspoken beneath it. Something about his talk had revived a forgotten faith. Suddenly, there he was, standing tall and striking in front of her, telling her Kamlesh had informed him she was the daughter of the famous historian whose work he knew well. Rehana caught her breath. She had a longing to reach up and fling her arms around him in sheer joy. She accepted the glass he took off a tray and handed her, saying, 'So should we not drink to your father?' This time she could have wept, but again for sheer joy. She had no idea what she was drinking, only that it was going to her head. She was talking animatedly to the German with the complete confidence of being understood and he was listening intently to what she was saying.

He invited her to stay on and dine with him and Gerda as Kamlesh was doing. They ate duck l'orange and other delectable dishes selected by him from the French menu. Superbly dined and wined, their talk drifted, unserious, unhurried. Franz turned vaguely philosophical.

'Purity,' he said, 'does not exist. It is a chimera, a dangerous, absurd imagining. No one and nothing is just one thing. Blood, culture, our past, our present, they are all mixed. Did Italy bring noodles to China or the other way round? Is a summer's day the temperature on the thermometer or is it a breeze, a bird, a butterfly…'

'He gets like that,' said Gerda lovingly,

slipping her arm through his and rubbing her cheek against his shirt sleeve, 'especially after such a meal.'

The band was playing nostalgic old favourites. Couples on the dance floor were in slow slumberous motion, dancing cheek to cheek. The crooner at the mike twitched her hips to the beat and huskily confessed:

When love walks in
And takes you for a spin
Ooo la la la, c'est magnifique!
And when once more he whispers 'Je t'adore'
C'est magnifique!

They agreed it was the perfect ending to Franz's book launch.

~

Aruna had brought a copy of Arati Ashwin's cookbook to show them at their book get-together. It was a present from a friend and clearly a collector's item. They passed it around. Rehana's hand glided over the pearly texture of its pages and its mouthwatering illustrations of unheard-of desserts.

'She won't be travelling for a while,' Aruna informed them. 'She's expecting. It was in the papers. It said she already has three but that Baba Ghanshyam who's advising on culture has called on patriotic Hindus to have at least five and she wants to set an example.'

'What do you think of your lot being told to stay pregnant? Looks like your Ghanshyam Baba and my Pope see eye to eye on womb control,' Lily said.

'Actually it's nothing new,' Rehana reflected, 'Wombs have been controlled by popes and imams and husbands since time began. By governments too. What about China's one-child policy that made women report their periods every month?'

'It's crazy,' said Lily, but it reminded her to tell them her news. Arati Ashwin had heard she designed elegant wear for an exclusive boutique that had its own outlet in Harrods. She had come to the boutique that morning and asked Lily to design a glamorous maternity wardrobe for her. She said pregnant women didn't have to look dowdy and saris were all wrong with all that cloth bunched up around one's middle. Looking glamorous would encourage women to have more babies.

Nandini called them to attention. She poured Flowery Orange Pekoe and they got on to the novel Lily had chosen. It was a new one by a feminist author about a woman in search of orgasm. Jennie hadn't realized what she was missing until she and her husband went to Rome on a holiday and saw Bernini's statue of Santa Teresa d'Avila. Rick who wasn't much of a sightseer and was good and ready for beer and lunch, took a brief look and strolled on.

Jennie hung back as she always did, wanting to get her sightseeing's money's worth. She fetched the tourist booklet out of her shoulder bag and found the page about the sixteenth-century nun. It informed her this was a must-see sculpture. It was Bernini's masterwork. Here it is then. The marble nun appears to be leaning way back in a swoon with one foot dangling off the platform she's sitting on. Her eyes are half closed and her mouth is half open. The guide book spelled out the swoon in Santa Teresa's own words: 'The pain was so strong that it made me utter several moans; and so excessive was the sweetness caused me by this intense pain that one can never wish it to cease...' Evidently Jesus Christ had promised her, 'If I had not created heaven, I would create it for you alone,' and here it is, heaven on earth for her alone.

A nun of all people, for Pete's sake, had this delirious dementing surrender to passion, never mind that it was only for Jesus Christ: 'Her body and spirit are in the throes of rapture,' read Jennie, 'happiness and pain alternating in a fearful fiery all-consuming glow. Such is her ecstasy in climax that her body is literally lifted up before it falls unconscious.' If this was orgasm, Jennie hadn't had one, nothing like. She was very thoughtful as she caught up with Rick and all through their spaghetti carbonara.

The rest of the novel tells of Jennie's adventures in pursuit of ecstasy. There are lovers and there are orgasms. Delicious outer ones, inner ones that take her by storm, on and off furniture and flat on the floor. And then there's that unexpected one arriving after what she had thought was the final one. Jennie is never exactly in the 'throes' of the nun's rapture but near enough. Jennie is Jennie-in-Wonderland.

'What really got me about the story,' said Lily, 'is how cheery it is all the way through. Nothing happens to interfere with the glorious time she's having. I found that exhilarating, and quite uplifting.'

Nandini, incredulous, asked, 'What's uplifting about it?'

'The contrast, of course. Women trudge behind men, they eat after men, they get less to eat than men, they do pujas for men, they stay hungry keeping fasts for men, they get killed before they're born, they are divorced at the drop of a hat, they can't leave home except in thick black shrouds, and they'd better be Virgin Marys or else.' Lily paused, then she said, 'And if that isn't enough, they get butchered to prevent them from having orgasms. No clitoris, no orgasm. What a life. So three cheers for Jennie.'

Silencing though that last horrifying fact was, Nandini, who had to get back to her office to oversee a wedding order, brought attention back to the book. She didn't know why feminist writers had to exaggerate so much to make their point. There was no need to give Jennie that many lovers. One or two would have sounded more convincing. And all those acrobatic goings-on with arms and legs thrown about and wound around in who-cares abandon were a bit much. Not a word about Rick while Jennie was whooping it up. What must the poor man have been going through?

'What do you think, Rehana?'

Rehana had been thinking of the unfairness of it, the nun having it all without stirring, so it was the power of imagination yet again, wasn't it? But that aside, all those acrobatics made Lady Chatterley sound positively stodgy and staid. Sex had come a long way since Lady Chatterley. It showed how much literary times had changed, and that sometimes things did change for the better.

For Aruna the most unconvincing part of the novel was Jennie and Rick staying married as if nothing had happened. 'It's preposterous. It would be impossible in real life.'

'I don't know about that,' countered Lily blandly. 'After all, Jennie and Rick are terribly fond of each other. Why should they break up? And adultery never breaks up a marriage, only knowing about it does.'

After this conclusion, Lily added, displaying her satisfaction with a book she had thoroughly enjoyed reading, 'Come to think of it, it's the story of holy matrimony, only the other way round.'

~

Rehana got home to find Abdul watering the well-weeded little lawn and the flower beds in bloom on two sides of it where he had planted a mismatching riot of flowers, tall and tiny, sturdy and fragile, delicate pastels alongside glaring reds and purples. It looked like a state of barely controlled chaos. Tiger lilies towering over phlox would leave any gardener in shock. Abdul was very pleased with it, marvelling at what had come through the earth at his bidding.

Her parents had built this house in the days when prices in this coveted area were affordable and she had grown up in it. With Vineet in the foreign service, they were out of India for most of their married life until illness cut short his career. They were both walkers and one of the pleasures of being posted abroad had been discovering an unknown city on foot. In Vineet's spare time they had taken walks through unfamiliar street sights and sounds, stopped for coffee or a bite to eat at a sidewalk café and sat there a while, complete in each other's company. The moments she could bear to remember were moments such as these.

The illness that took him was stealthy and ruthless. A creeping paralysis disabled him by degrees until the only movement left to him was to nod his head. At the very last, his face immobilized, he could only blink. She had given thanks for his death when it came and she could let herself break down into helpless unstoppable mourning. Grief is long-lasting, rebellious, everlasting. But like everything that becomes familiar, one starts noticing it less.

Every mourner before her must have wondered if there was life after death, or as some believed, life after life—farfetched, pointless speculations that were no earthly use to those who were left behind. Last week she had been at Lily's for Easter brunch on the day they celebrated the resurrection of Christ. It reminded her of an Easter in Ireland when she and Vineet had gone to church with friends and heard Handel's *Messiah* performed. Gooseflesh had prickled her arms and the church itself had seemed to burst its confines, hard-pressed to contain the majesty of the Hallelujah chorus. Who knew for sure if the crucified prisoner called Jesus of Nazareth had really risen from the tomb? Had he really appeared in the flesh to his disciples on the road to Emmaeus? Had anyone else seen him? But a church had risen for all to see and this victorious rapture had risen for all to hear in praise of him.

This may be all we could ever know about life after death.

Hers was the last house in this tree-shaded lane off the main road. It used to be quiet. Now, with more cars than the road could hold, the incessant rumble and roar of machinery in motion reached her. Stalled in their tracks, a manic bray of horns demanded motion where none was possible. And there were nearer night noises. A rowdy argument, a street quarrel, a drunken brawl. Were voices pitched louder in the night or did they sound louder because it was night? One night a ruckus outside the neighbouring house compelled her out of bed and to her bedroom window. The couple next door were home late from a party. The woman being flung against the iron gate was teetering on her stiletto heels. The street light shone on her sequinned sari. Her husband was slapping her expertly with the back of his hand swinging back and forth across her face until she lost her balance. The next morning she had smiled prettily and waved her jewelled fingers at Rehana through the window of her silver-grey chauffeur-driven palace on wheels. Rehana had waved back.

Around mid-morning next day Cyrus's car drove in. She ran downstairs to be enveloped in his bear hug, and they sat by the garden wall under the shade of the cassia's blossoming branches. It was unusual for Cyrus to arrive unannounced in the middle of a working day. Abdul came out, was given a friendly punch in the midriff and told to provide coffee.

Cyrus owned the art gallery he had inherited from his father and it was Batlivala senior who, in the explosion of energies after independence, had given his controversial opinion: 'Art is what kicks where it hurts' and had championed breakaway art. He had bought and exhibited Nikhil's early work and they had become fast friends. Cyrus, not just his father's son, had become a discerning discoverer in his own right and was entitled to some smugness on that account, but he refused to take himself seriously or to be serious about anything. In Cyrus-fashion he called his art-spotting his poor substitute for not being able to paint. As a schoolboy, he had been driven by a desperation to draw. His drawing master and Papa Batlivala had done their darndest to make an artist of him, but, alas, Cyrus baba had been a hopeless case.

Abdul brought coffee and requested Cyrus to call him Morari Lal. Rehana had to explain why.

'I know the place he would have been sent to,' said Cyrus, 'I've been there. Housing they call it, but it's tenements crammed together, with rooms no bigger than holes in the wall. I went there to find a boy. His name is Hanif. I came across a painting of his quite by chance and I had to find him. He works in a scullery in an eating place nearby. Will he have to spend the rest of his life living in that rathole, washing dirty degchis and plates for a living? That boy is an artist. He must paint. I've got to get him out of there. It's not going to be easy now that he's been listed and already removed to that ghetto.'

The Batlivalas were a wealthy family, and like his father, Cyrus helped and nurtured young and needy artists. To dilute the distressing situation he had described, she said lightly, 'Why haven't you been listed, Cyrus? You're an outsider.'

He wagged an admonishing finger at her. 'You're forgetting history, Rehana. Outsiders were the noisy conquering kind. We smart fellows slipped in quietly much earlier and since we're a dwindling handful we don't count. Actually, who's even heard of us? Let me tell you about my grandpa who was a penniless nobody in London when the First World War started and being the loyal chap he was, he lined up to be recruited to fight for King and empire. When his turn came and he had given his name, the recruiting sergeant at the desk bawled out, "What's your religion?" and grandpa said, "Parsee."

"You mean RC?"

'Grandpa repeated "Parsee".

'The sergeant turned to the uniformed minion standing by his desk, "What in bleeding Hades is that?" to be told, "Ee's one of them blokes wot worships the sun." But to get to the point, dear girl, Nikhil's anniversary is coming up, that is, of his first exhibition with us, and I think we should exhibit what we have of his works again along with the other progressives.'

She gave her enthusiastic approval and said she would be along to help in any way she could.

Cyrus rang a few days later. 'About the boy, I made an appointment with the DCT. There are so many initials floating around, you may not know this stands for Director of Cultural Transformation. He's also in charge of racial purity so the ghetto comes under him. I went to see him yesterday in that new glass-fronted high-rise and I was taken straight through past the front room where hordes were waiting to see him, to his office at the back. It looks out on a spreading lawn with a sprinkler watering the greenest grass and the reddest roses you ever saw. His office was all peace and light. Like a painting by Vermeer, I swear. A bowl of purple pansies on his desk. Pictures of their heroes on the wall behind him. And he couldn't have been more gracious. He gave me cardamom tea and said he's sensitive to aromas, cardamom and other spices, but above all to the seasonal perfumes of his garden. He had inherited his sensitivity. From your father? I asked him. From the ages, he said with a smile. The inheritance of skills is the crowning glory of caste. It fine-tunes each skill to its finest, which is why he can tell one flower's scent from another with his eyes closed, even one rose from another, a yellow from a pink or a white. Well, after that he said he had heard of my good father and knew of my own devotion to art. He wanted to know what he could do for me. When I told him he assured me my concern for this person, whoever he was, was truly praiseworthy and so typical of my community which cared for its own with such well-known compassion and now for this person who was not of my community. But this person whoever he was, was well settled in the housing estate set up for his community, so there was no need to worry on that score. It was a complete arrangement with its own market and shops where they had their own tailors, butchers, barbers and others of their own community to serve their community. People like to be among their own kind, and moving them out of the city had been a safety measure for their own good, with feeling running so high against them. "We cannot forget the pain of invasions, Mr Batlivala, the Turks, Mongols, Mughals, foreigners who interrupted our Hindu history. You may say we are now engaged in wiping out that painful memory and returning our nation by all possible means to its racial and religious purity. Is that not plain justice? That is the cultural transformation we are bringing about.

"Notwithstanding all that, Mr Batlivala, I would have done my best to grant your request, only now the matter of a separate estate for his community has passed into law so with deep regret my hands are tied."

'Then, Rehana, he got up and walked with me to the door and out to the verandah and pointed with pride to the red rose beds and in case I hadn't noticed them, the blush-pink beauties rambling up the garden wall. "Other than this matter if there is anything else I can do…" So we said Bharat Mata ki Jai to each other and I came away.'

'Well then,' she said resignedly, 'there's nothing to be done.'

'I've already done what had to be done. I abducted the boy. I went there, put him and his mother and their belongings into my car and drove off. There was nobody around.'

She might have guessed Cyrus would find his

own way out of an intractable problem but she had not been prepared for law-breaking. Ignoring her alarm he said, 'Hanif is safe with me for the moment but I'll have to find him and his mother a place somewhere soon where he can earn as well as be able to paint. His mother is a tailor and has her sewing machine with her so she will be able to carry on her tailoring.'

'But Cyrus—'

'No buts, Rehana, think ahead,' and he rang off.

~

Nandini was thinking of choosing non-fiction as her book choice for a change, and then for a real change why not ask the author to come and talk to them?

'But four people isn't exactly an audience,' she admitted ruefully, 'so it wouldn't be worthwhile for the writer. No one would come.'

Aruna agreed it was out of the question. 'Authors can be tricky about their importance. At the festival here last year there was one who refused to share the stage with another author. He wanted to perform solo. One would think he'd created the world instead of a book.'

She was a Member of Parliament and brought books that would not have otherwise come to their notice. 'There's an interesting one I wish we could read. The review said it was about the very latest research on populations and that ours like most others has come out of migrations. In other words we're not a pure race polluted by later comers. The writer has been arrested.'

'What for? Under what law can they do that?' they clamoured.

'Under the law against dangerous thoughts. And he's in solitary confinement so that he doesn't infect others. Some of us in Parliament are working for his release.'

'If there's anything I can do. . .' said Rehana

and Aruna nodded, saying she would be in touch.

They would have parted unhappily if Rehana, accustomed to reconnecting with ordinary life after news of this kind, had not had an inspiration for Nandini's book choice. If Kamlesh had the time she was sure he would be willing to talk to them about the Taj though he was still working on it.

'Perfect,' said Nandini, 'he's a friend of yours, Rehana, please ask him. Frankly I'm ready for something romantic, some true love after all that Jennie business.'

Nandini ruled out Flowery Orange Pekoe. Men liked proper tea. And cake and sandwiches for a busy man, a diplomat who would be sparing them his valuable time.

Kamlesh said he would be glad to come and try out his perspective on their little group of discerning readers. He arrived with a few folded pages of his manuscript tucked into his trouser pocket and Aruna's notion of authorial airs and graces was quickly dispelled. Warmly welcomed and directed to the chair Nandini knew men liked, he began by telling them about his fascination for architecture because of the powerful feelings it could evoke. So he had been drawn to finding out what he could about that building of buildings, the Taj Mahal. It was built in the grand tradition of Mughal architecture, and like all their architecture it was massive, it was spectacular, it took your breath away just to stand and marvel at it from a distance. But this one was exceptional even for the Mughals, in its attention to the minutest detail. Contemporary Persian write-ups about the Taj waxed lyrical about its marble surfaces inlaid with floral designs and precious stones, the gold and silver that illuminated the tomb; the famed calligraphy of Amanat Khan on vast marble expanses of it, not to mention the size of the fortune spent on erecting it. An awe-struck Persian poet had written: 'Since the very moment of creation, who till now has seen an edifice like this?' And if all that wasn't exceptional enough, unlike any other building on earth it was a monument to married love and owed its existence to a bereaved Emperor's inconsolable sorrow.

'So,' said Kamlesh, 'It was that difference from all other buildings, its emotional aspect, that intrigued me.'

He smoothed his crumpled pages on his lap and read out what an agent of the East India Company, Peter Mundy, had had to say about it: 'The Kinge is now building a sepulcher for his late deceased Queen Tage Moholl, whome he dearely affected, having had by her nine or ten children and thought in her life tyme to use noe other women (which is strange if true considering their libertie in that kinde.) The buildinge is begun… Gold and silver esteemed common Metall, and Marble but as ordinarie stones…'

Kamlesh had to correct Peter Mundy. 'Mumtaz

Mahal had fourteen children in her nineteen years of marriage. Seven of them died and she herself died giving birth to the fourteenth.'

It was a tragic ending to a great love story, he said, but apart from that known fact, facts had been hard to come by. There were histories of Shah Jahan written by court historians because the Emperor wanted to go down in history, as his grandfather Babur had through his Turkish memoirs and his father Jahangir through his Persian memoirs. But the trouble with courtiers writing histories was that you drowned in their language. The Shah Jahan chronicles were so fulsome and flooded with praise of the Emperor's reign that you couldn't tell fact from fairytale: his 'sky-touching edifices, heart-pleasing gardens through which Hindustan has taken on immeasurable splendour, armies as numerous as the stars', and of course his noble character, his great benevolence and so on. The Empress was described as 'that holy-natured one of angelic character' and more such praise. And naturally no court history had anything to say about the private side of imperial life. But glimpses of it filtered into seventeenth century Europe through the tales carried by European travellers. These might well have been based on rumour and juicy court gossip of which there was no lack, but not entirely. There must have been something more substantial to go on. One widespread rumour that titillated Europe by the end of 1631, six months after Mumtaz Mahal's death, was of the Emperor's incestuous relations with their daughter, Jahanara.

'Yes, I know,' said Kamlesh, glancing up at the dismay he was facing, 'but we can't ignore it. Here's what the French traveller Bernier had to say,' and he read it out: 'The elder daughter of Chah-Jehan was very handsome, of lively parts, and passionately beloved by her father.'

'It was public knowledge that she was his favourite child,' said Kamlesh, 'and that her father had given her half the wealth left by her mother, and her six siblings had had to share the other half. As for the incest rumour, it must have been true. Bernier says the Emperor consulted the Mullahs about it: "Rumour has it that he rested on the decision of the Mullahs, or doctors of their law. According to them, it would have been unjust to deny the King the privilege of gathering fruit from the tree he had himself planted." So it seems the Mullahs actually gave him the go-ahead to sleep with his daughter. We can take it that it was true.' Kamlesh looked up again and said apologetically, 'Well, there it is. And apart from incest with Jahanara, there must have been plenty of gossip about his Majesty's morals for European travellers to be able to report it in such detail. According to the Italian, Manucci, the Emperor was known for the ways he indulged his sexual appetites "as if the only thing Shah Jahan cared for was the search for women to serve his pleasure," and that "his intimacy with the wives of his nobles was notorious." Manucci claimed he had authentic information: "I was admitted on familiar terms to this house, and I was deep in the confidence of the privileged ladies and eunuchs in her (the Empress's) service." He certainly left us what reads like an insider's account.'

Kamlesh went on to read it out: 'For the greater satisfaction of his lusts Shah Jahan ordered the erection of a large hall, twenty cubits long and eight cubits wide, adorned throughout with great mirrors. The gold alone cost fifteen millions of rupees, not including the enamel work and precious stones, of which no account was kept. On the ceiling of the said hall, between one mirror and another, were strips of gold richly ornamented with jewels. At the corners of the mirrors hung great clusters of pearls, and the walls were of jasper stone. All this expenditure was made so that he might obscenely observe himself and his favourite women.'

After more readings from European observers' accounts Kamlesh put down his papers and said,

'Well, I'm sorry but that's the way it seems to be. Maybe the truth lies somewhere between the court histories and the travellers' tales. But it's reasonable to assume that our inconsolable Emperor was not a one-woman man. How could he have been, with two other wives, hundreds in his harem, and the pick of whoever he fancied at court or in a crowd. Men who occupy thrones and have a free run are not known to be one-woman men. Witness our maharajas before they became ordinary citizens like the rest of us. Lechery has no religion.'

'All the same,' said Nandini, 'What a let-down. All those mirrors.'

'There are different sides to all of us,' Kamlesh offered by way of explanation to lighten the gloom, 'No one is all of a piece. They say Mussolini played hide-and-seek with his children and liked nothing better than to gather his family around the piano for sing-songs. Hitler was known to enjoy operetta, "The Student Prince",

"The Chocolate Soldier" and the rest. "The Merry Widow" was his favourite. For all we know he may have whirled his partners around to the "Merry Widow" waltz at Nazi merry-makings. Can't you just see him?'

They couldn't. The jolly side of Mussolini and Hitler did not make up for their disillusionment with Shah Jahan.

'When all is said and done,' said Kamlesh, 'There's really no doubt that Mumtaz Mahal was his true beloved. The palace and the entire realm knew it. It was the talk of the town. She even accompanied him to his battlefields. A legend like that doesn't spring out of nothing. Whatever he did in front of all those mirrors, with her he must have made love as love should be made. And after all, to end all doubt, there's the Taj Mahal.'

'Besides,' he continued, 'she was very much an ordinary mortal too, not the holy and angelic image of her in court histories.' He read what the well-informed Manucci had had to say about her less angelic side:

'Finding himself undisputed King of Hindustan, Shah Jahan was compelled to make war against the Portuguese of Hugli, for this was demanded by Queen Taj Mahal from whom the Portuguese had carried off two of her slave girls. He sent against them the general Qasim Khan who seized five thousand souls, among them some Augustinian and Jesuit fathers and carried them off to court. God willed that before they arrived there, the Queen Taj Mahal should die. There can be no doubt that in her lifetime she would have ordered the whole of them to be cut into pieces after great tortures. All the same, they did not escape a sufficient amount of suffering.'

After this final revelation there was nothing more to be said, so tea was poured.

'Someone should write about the women in harems,' said Kamlesh, accepting another slice of cake. 'There they were, captive for the rest of their lives. Hens in a coop being fed and fattened for roasting. Waiting for a summons that might never come. What do you suppose they did? Become lesbian lovers? Have hi-jinks with the eunuchs? Go crazy? Die of boredom? What women have had to go through is mindboggling. No wonder they've said enough is enough.'

After he had gone Lily declared, 'He's a real sweetie. What's his wife like?'

Rehana said they were separated. 'Gayatri is in the foreign service too. They kept being posted continents apart, and it was too much of a strain on their relationship. But they're on the best of terms.'

'Well, now let me show you my maternity creation,' said Lily.

She eased it out of its tissue wrapping, shook it delicately and held it up with the tips of her thumbs and forefingers. Their loud acclaim told Lily how exquisite it was. She pointed out its features—the silky softness and gossamer lightness of the fabric, so that its extra folds in front would hardly be felt on the growing belly bulge. Circularly cut, it curved gracefully from shoulder to ankle, its downward flow changing colour from violet to a glacial blue and ending in a fashionable uneven hemline.

They congratulated Lily on her inspired creation, saying sadists must have designed women's clothes through the ages. Fully clothed through her labour, Marie Antoinette had gasped and groaned behind a screen with the whole French court sitting on the other side chit-chatting while they waited for the newborn cry. It was the custom, to make sure the genuine royal article was being delivered and not a substitute smuggled in.

Lily folded her garment away. 'On the strength of this one, Mrs Ashwin is going to recommend me to her pregnant friends in Daughters of the Cultural Transformation. They're all pledged to five. I'll be making a fortune.'

'I hope you're going to take us out to lunch,' said Aruna.

'This deserves a cocktail celebration. I'll take us to the new Nirvana bar,' Lily promised.

~

The Rohners, back from their trip to the south, came to Rehana's to say goodbye, Kamlesh with them. He opened the bottle of champagne they had brought, a farewell gift from Nalin Ashwin. Arati hoped Gerda had shopped without a care because their excess baggage would be no problem. It would be flown to Mumbai in the Ashwins' private carrier and taken to the ship.

'It is a puzzle to me that readers do not understand the seriousness of my humour,' said Franz. 'Here is Nalin Ashwin making an honoured guest of me because he thinks my books about revolutions, including his favourite German one, are clever comedies when in fact they show the evil that men do in the name of revolution.'

They were full of their trip, Franz remarking on its architectural and historic splendours, and Gerda, ever the romantic, saying 'To stand on the tip of India is to be shocked by the sight of the ocean. What sight can compare with that for us land-locked people?'

Franz commiserated with Rehana about her father's disappeared books.

'The banning and burning of people, of books, how it repeats itself.'

He had persuaded the public library at home to open a wing for banned books. It was a great success, with books from the last hundred years. He wished her Papa's could have been added to it. Rehana could hardly contain her excitement. Nor could he when Abdul brought up the two leather suitcases and banged the dust off them. Franz and Gerda conferred in rapid German and Kamlesh was asked to go with Gerda to buy a new suitcase, but immediately, before the shops closed.

'It will be our excess baggage,' Franz told

Rehana while they waited, 'It will travel with us on our cruise and then home. I will stay in touch with you, Rehana.' He held out a hand and squeezed hers.

After the festivity of their champagne toasts to each other the room was very quiet.

Franz said, 'Your father's books must be preserved because he is telling how a civilization came to be, all that was happening in those times, the science, the music, the art, the intellectual life, the ordinary life in that long transition from ancient times.'

'But I suppose that was the trouble, Franz, and that's why they've been got rid of. There wasn't enough about the invasions. The Muslim invasions have been called the bloodiest in our history, some say the bloodiest in all history.'

Franz waved a dismissive hand. 'Can bloodshed then be measured? What we know for certain is there has been no shortage of it anywhere, and slaughters have surpassed each other everywhere. What is there to pick and choose between trampling a man to death under elephants' feet or disembowelling him alive? Or nailing six thousand rebels to crosses along the Appian Way as the Romans did? Or Hiroshima and Nagasaki? From far back until today it is a competition for who is the most barbaric and we have not seen the end of it.' It was his business to be in touch with ongoing atrocities for his researches.

What he had said made her tell him about the work she was doing, saying she had not realized she would be haunted by the images it left indelibly stamped on her. If only she could wipe them out, if only for a little while.

'This you can do, Rehana. Like the climber who grips every toehold on the cliffside, so must we learn to do. Enjoy the chocolate melting on your tongue, sing *La Vie En Rose*, walk among your Himalayan pines, and then there is fresh asparagus…'

She couldn't help laughing.

Kamlesh and Gerda came back jubilant with their find. The new suitcase was the largest and latest in elegant air travel. It had some room left after the books had been fitted into it. Gerda said she would lay her nighties and beachwear on top along with a copy of *Mein Kampf* just in case it was opened but of course it would not be opened on the Ashwins' private carrier.

When prolonged goodbyes had been said, Franz turned back from the car to add in his decisive manner, 'We will meet again.'

~

The Batlivala Gallery was a circular building facing the road. The courtyard had wrought-iron chairs and tables under garden umbrellas. Bougainvilleas were in exuberant bloom. Indoors there were cushioned chairs, no hard benches, for long and leisurely gazing, banishing the notion that a work of art is watched standing up and forward marching to the next one like a military manoeuvre. Seated, alone with the work, time stops. Then comes the illumined transporting moment that art bestows upon its gazers. Cyrus had hung the paintings far apart, each enshrined in its privileged space as befitted the celebrated art of a renaissance, each differently framed, uniquely itself and not just part of a 'movement'. Cyrus had been particular about that. Rehana surveyed the arrangement with satisfaction. She had told him she would stay back and look around the exhibition before joining him in his office. It was opening day when most viewers were likely to come. She felt nearer happiness than she had for a long time now that Papa's books were safely away and Nikhil's work was on view. She stood in front of one, reacquainting herself with it. Light flickered, flashed, leapt through deepening dark, expanding before her eyes into a lightning-lit landscape in the breath-held instant before the night sky explodes in a tumultuous storm.

She heard people arriving. A rock thudded past her ear into the stormy sky and crashed near her foot. She cried out as a knife pierced the landscape and stuck there. She turned in panic to see missiles flying straight as arrows to their mark. Something razor-sharp ripped through her sari. Something solid hit her head and sent her staggering to fall on shredded glass and splintered wood. Somewhere far away Cyrus was shouting through the din. Minutes later she felt herself being helped up, steered backward to the wall and lowered onto a sofa. Stunned and unable to lift her head she saw polished black patent leather shoes. A soothing voice spoke. 'Stay here, shrimati-ji, and you will come to no harm.' The shoes went away. The bombardment raged on. Raw pain stabbed one side of her and stung her swollen face. Her head throbbed. Her fingers came away wet with the blood on her cheek. Her uninjured eye made out gunny sacks in the rubble, empty of what they had carried. Thick dust hovered over battered frames, scissored canvases and broken furniture. The job completed, they piled their hammers, knives and shears back into their sacks and took their leave.

Cyrus had come to sit beside her. 'I phoned the police when it started,' he said, 'That was an hour ago. We must get you to a doctor.' Rehana gestured at the wreckage on the floor. 'All that later,' he said. Sitting speechless in his car she recalled the polished black shoes. No long white hooded robes, no high white pointed hats, no burning cross. It did not need a Klu Klux Klan to terrorize. Franz had said evil is an ordinary thing. Nice people, fond fathers, doting husbands do these things.

Cyrus had let Aruna know she would not be at their book get-together that week. There would be no book meeting, Aruna had assured him. All three of them came to see her, shocked by his account of the savage attack and the bandaged sight of her. Aruna had told her brother about it immediately and Hari, who worked under the DCT, had reported it to him.

'Hari says the DCT was terribly upset to hear what had happened to you.'

'Not to me,' Rehana spoke as best she could, 'I just happened to be in the line of fire.'

The DCT had expressed his sincere regret to Cyrus for the damage and the loss of his valuable property. Unfortunately, he said, national feeling once roused was hard to control. It had come to the notice of those men that the painters were Communists but they should have asked Mr Batlivala not to hold the exhibition, then this would not have happened. It was very reprehensible. Mr Batlivala must report it. The law would take its course.

'I know. Cyrus told me all that,' said Rehana, horror trapped like her voice and her tears behind bandaging.

'Rehana, it's no good being in the line of fire. You could have been killed,' Nandini was speaking urgently for all of them, 'As it is, the work you do is so depressing. Why do you have to be involved in things you can do nothing about?'

She didn't know why, unless it was hearing her mother say the unknown, unseen comradeship of other prisoners had kept her going, a hundred thousand of them in that last campaign not counting those who had been fined, flogged, or shot. How could they have borne it without the thought of each other?

'That's all very well but you mustn't go on with your work,' her friends insisted, 'Why did you get into it in the first place?'

Because people are tortured for refusing to agree the moon shines by day and the sun by night, because there are cells—hells—for the torture known as solitary confinement, because hanging doesn't break a neck, it cracks it and slowly strangles. And because of what happens up the road and around the corner. All this remained unsaid. They knew very well why she had started working with Asians Against Torture. It had started when she met the Indian group's founder at lunch at Kamlesh's house one day during the long emptiness after Vineet's death.

'But you take things too much to heart, Rehana. After all, what can you do about it?'

'We do what we can and it's little enough, even if it's only making public what people all over Asia including ourselves are going through.'

'Like what?' demanded Lily.

An instance out of daily hundreds across the sprawl of Asia, where warlords, ruling tyrants and madness ran amok, making free with human flesh? But she needed an example to convince them.

'In Uzbekistan,' she brought out finally, 'people who oppose Karimov get boiled in oil.'

They were aghast. 'It can't be. Not in this day and age.'

'And in Kazakhstan, Nazarbayev's torture chambers are just as fancy. We keep hoping other countries won't do business with them, but where there's all that oil and gas…' her voice trailed off.

In the violent world her work connected her with, whose actual acts of violence she had documented but not laid eyes on, she said her own accidental drubbing at the exhibition had at least given her a shadowy acquaintance with it. It was not what they wanted to hear. They got up to go, taking turns to put careful loving arms around her, and told her they would keep coming.

The bombardment came roaring back around Rehana. It had been as thorough as the razing of Guernica which had been cheerfully recorded as a rehearsal for the real thing. But here? What had brought matters to this pass? She brooded over the bombardment. There was not much else to do, immobilized and mummified as she was. Her sense of loss was searing. She had grown up in thrall to characters in books, on language that could desolate or exhilarate. She had discovered feelings she would not have known she had but for the beauty and power of paint. She remembered the first time she had heard the word 'painting' and thought it meant amazing. Nikhil was talking to her parents about his long-ago visit to Mexico where he had gone on holiday from university. He was recalling his sheer amazement. He had never seen paintings march across walls, move up and down huge high spaces, never known paintings could be stories inseparable from walls. The painter to whom he had an introduction was at the top of a wall-high ladder, at work where wall met ceiling.

As Nikhil told it: I am transfixed, looking up. My gaze is riveted to where intricate detail is holding its own undaunted by the sweep and size of the painted drama surrounding it. Finally the painter finishes and glances down. He puts his brush away and his bulky bulbous figure steps down the ladder, his back to me. Reaching the ground he turns around and his ugly face lights up, not at the sight of me, but when seeing me he exclaims 'India!' as if the sun has risen in all its glory around us. I am overwhelmed, not only because I am young and bedazzled in the presence of greatness, but because no other country has called an artist its most famous citizen, an artist whose wall paintings Mexicans trudge miles barefoot to see. Think Mexico and you think Diego. Think Mexico and you think art. I am at a loss for words but Diego Rivera is not. He is expecting me. The generosity of his welcome matches the breadth of his bulk, and it is not for me, an unknown Indian student but for the country I come from, where, as all the world knows, the most awesome reality is not the might of the British Viceroy or the guns of his King Emperor's occupying army but the man of whom Einstein has written: 'Generations to come, it may be, will scarce believe that such a one as this in flesh and blood walked upon this earth.' Think India and you think Gandhi.

Art is alive in the republic of Mexico. I am there at a time when artists meet, argue, quarrel. About real, surreal, abstract. Mural or easel? For the few or for the masses? Can art survive in Spain if the fascist Franco wins Spain? Has Lenin's revolution been bloodied and betrayed beyond repair by Stalin? Art is no reclusive ivory tower. It is passionate and political. In a struggle it takes sides. In this ambience, in such company, I hardly dare call myself an artist though that is what I know I am and the reason why I am here. Diego fans the flame in me. He points to the walls where he has painted two thousand years of Mexico's history from Aztec empire to Mexican Republic. It is all there, Aztec legends and splendours, Spain's barbarous conquest, the French and American invasions. All this is who we are, he says, and you have more thousand years for your walls. When I look puzzled about bestowing immortality on brute conquest, plunder and rape, he says it is our history so it is part of us. He points to the gringos on the wall and laughs. Where there is oil, he says, there comes the gringo! To me he commands: Go home and paint!

Would Nikhil's paintings have been saved, Rehana wondered, if he had painted murals? But once he was back home the fight for freedom had come first and jail took over. After that, undreamed of strokes on canvas took intoxicating flights from 'parampara' on the easel that served Nikhil as a wall, revealing us as creatures of our history. But wall or easel made no difference since the hardiest walls and highest mountains had not protected art. Machine guns had been trained on giant Buddhas in the Hindukush. Antique portals and pillars had been dynamited. Yet Franz insisted evil-doers are no different from the rest of us. They have brains, balls, veins like other men, no body part is missing, there is nothing you can single them out by. They are men who buy dolls for their children and light the candles on their birthday cakes. How do we know this, Rehana? In Nuremburg after the war, during trials of the men who had masterminded evils such as mankind had never seen, it surprised judges and onlookers that they looked, talked and behaved like ordinary men. This is how we know.

Catching up with her mail she found one from Franz saying Gerda had acquired a beautiful tan and on a 1920s dance night on the cruise they had learned to do the Bunny Hug. They had put on weight but did not regret it because the food had mocked abstemiousness and the Chinese had surpassed expectations. Out of the whole world's cuisine, Rehana, only the Chinese have excelled in the refined and subtle art of nuancing flavours. Nuance must be the secret at the heart of civilization. We in the West have lost the art.

Nandini came with grapes and cherries to speed her recovery and tactfully reminded Rehana to think about quitting Asians Against

Torture. A silent minute or so was usual now when talking was a bit of a strain, but Rehana's answer, when it came, only recalled the day she had first heard of it at Kamlesh's lunch. At the time, given Rehana's need for getting on with her life, Nandini admitted to the others afterwards, it had made sense. But it was doing her no good to go on with it. In casual conversation with a friend at the lunch that day Rehana had said the foreign service cut one off from the daily grind at home, diplomats were too far removed from it. The group's founder had interrupted tersely to assure her that we, here, were as far removed from what went on within shouting distance.

'Up the road or around the corner a man is being beaten bloody under interrogation,' he said. 'Another is stripped naked and kept standing naked for hours. Being dead at the end of it all is called suicide. And sexual savagery is everyday business. All this is news to you? That's what I mean.'

Loud laughter had burst out around them, a joke someone had told. Rehana could have joined in it herself. The repellant saga of treatment in police custody and the anger that had spelled it out had released her to a future she had forgotten existed, one that would occupy her usefully. In the beginning it had been no more than that. An opportunity came her way soon after when the group asked her to get the facts about a bicycle thief who had needlessly been kept in custody and only just released.

The garbage in the side street was no longer the mountain it had been. Sunk, scattered, spread, it was a stagnant stinking ocean in which skeletal cows and mangy dogs went fishing and ragged children dived diligently for pickings. The door of the dwelling opened an inch and another few inches to admit her sideways when she gave her name. A woman sat in a corner on the bare floor, knees drawn up, her arms hanging lifelessly over them. Her sari palla was pulled down over her face. A child lay on one of the two nivar cots. The haggard grey-faced man who had let Rehana in motioned her to the other sagging cot. Rehana sat down, unsure how to proceed. She had questions in mind and was ready to talk when he offered her tea, making a graceless interloper of her in the presence of timeless courtesy and putting him in charge in a curious reversal of their roles. Thanking him she declined and asked if she could talk to the person who had been released from custody. His eyes indicated the inert child and her questions were not needed. The man spoke: My boy took the bicycle from a public parking place. He is only twelve years old. It was just for a joyride. He left it somewhere further up the road where the police found it and returned it to its owner. That is all but the constable took him in. It was a hotel room the constable took him to, where he dragged his pants off, threw him across the bed and did the unspeakable upon his helpless body.

Her mind recoiled from the toneless clarity of his recital. The struggling child pinned down, his arms spread wide, a battalion astride him. In a futile attempt to shut out the image she took out her notebook and wrote down the father's and child's names. Mohammed Hamid and Jamal. We will do all we can, she promised. First a complaint would have to be made.

'No complaint can be made,' Mohammed Hamid informed her, recognizing a novice in these matters. 'They called a doctor to examine my boy. The doctor said there is no injury. Then he pointed to the constable and said to my boy, "Did this man torture you?"'

Rehana saw the constable standing, his legs immovable as tree trunks planted solidly apart, empowered by the authority of khaki, the child cowering. In answer to the doctor she could hear Jamal mumbling 'No'.

Mohammed Hanif's eyes were on her face.

He was making sure she had understood that fear was useful in resolving these cases.

~

Aruna was not going ahead with selecting a book for discussion. They were all still shaken by the bombardment on the exhibition and the thought that Rehana could have been killed. They took turns coming over to keep her company, and lavished their time, their work time, to help out with jobs that needed to be done. Rehana felt the familiar comfort of living off the soundness and normalcy of their lives as she always had, but now increased a hundredfold by all they were doing for her. Her godlessness, confirmed by what the human race was made to go through—no miracles of rescue forthcoming—had accustomed her to ruling out divine help. The miracle, as ever before in history, was human help and workaday human love.

Aruna brought avocados grown on a farm in her parliamentary constituency and some news. 'Hari says preparations are on for culture week. The Ashwins will be giving a party to announce it. You must come, Rehana, your bandages will be off by then and it's just as well to keep up with what's going on. Hari will send you an invitation. Lily says she isn't interested and Nandini won't be able to make it.'

But her first outing took her back to work, to the government office where the group had made an appointment for her. The government official looked up from the papers on his desk with an air of having been interrupted at work. Then, ah yes, Asians Against Torture is well respected. Fine work. He was sorry to have kept her waiting. Rehana said the organization wished to make an urgent plea on behalf of an asylum seeker beyond Afghanistan who faced certain death by beheading or by slower means if he was arrested. He was in hiding, awaiting word of permission to enter India.

The official looks grave and solicitous. Who does not value human life but asylum is a delicate, not merely a humanitarian issue, not a decision to be taken in haste, it takes time to ascertain credentials, who is this man?

He is a poet, an old man, and there is no time.

I understand, says the official, but we have diplomatic relations with his country, a region of strategic importance to us, not done to interfere in their internal affairs, would lead to serious political and economic consequences, can she guarantee this man is not engaged in subversive activity, treason takes many forms.

Rehana says he writes about hills, skies, meadows, of his love for his countryside. He reads his poems to his people. There are times and places where poetry gives heart and hope, the only hope.

Quite so, says the man at the desk that separates their consciences, but that is not the information we require, this being as I said a delicate matter.

'If he is captured they will do to him what they do to those whom they take prisoner,' she says.

With the detachment she has drilled herself in, she describes in short sentences the tortures in use upon body, mind and soul. The official's expression of startled disgust and acute discomfort makes it clear this degree of accuracy is hardly necessary. Most unpleasant if true. Much as we decry such treatment, if true, we cannot make an exception in his case without further investigation because if an exception is made in his case it will open the floodgates to asylum seekers. I do not have the authority to give you an immediate answer and we will study the report you have given us but I must urge you not to expect an answer in the near future owing to the factors we must consider in our relations with a friendly country as also the diplomatic correctness of the stand we take and now if you will excuse me I am already late for an official luncheon.

Out on the pavement she looked at her watch to begin the fearful vigil of counting the hours, twenty-four, forty-eight at most, until their thorough combing captured him. In times when economic consequences were more delicate than frail old skin and bone there was only one prayer. She closed her eyes and prayed. For beheading, not dismembering. For swift, not atrocious dragged-out death.

Her second outing a few days later was to Nandini's where they foregathered to talk about Aruna's book choice and life resumed its interrupted rhythm. Whatever was tearing the world apart, all loveliness last looked upon no longer there to see, here they could drink a tranquil cup of tea at peace in the enduring light of literature.

Aruna had chosen a novel just out about the despair of a lifetime condemned to filth removal.

He cannot wash his fingers clean of it nor scrape nor scour its abominable odours off his skin nor rid his nostrils of the foul inherited stench which is the curse of lifetimes that are spent skinning dead cows, handling human waste and living steeped in its filth. It is the malodorous breath he inhales, it circulates with his blood, it clogs his pores and lodges in the marrow of his bones. In desperation he seeks cure after cure and then is told the love of God will cure him. But having been unloved by God these past millenia he seeks the love of a goddess. Her bewitching young breasts, narrow thighs and beguiling slenderness receive and take possession of him. Ardour and appetite he has known but not the exquisite refinements of her five thousand-year-old embrace or such torrential surrenders to passion as at her lightest touch. When she eases him off herself he rises cleansed, purified, and liberated to live and breathe as other men do, touch and be touched like them.

Nandini said thankfully, 'A real love story at last.'

'An unreal one,' Aruna reminded them, 'Only a fantasy could free him of his occupation and give him a life of dignity. It's far from real.'

Rehana said, 'According to Picasso, art is a lie that makes us realize the truth.'

'Picasso didn't know us. The truth is this man couldn't have sex, much less a raging affair with a woman outside his stench-range. Nor could he decide on a filth-free life for himself. Even in the story he doesn't have a name. He's "he" all the way through. He's nobody and nothing. And caste makes sure he stays that way, forever untouchable.'

'Whether it could happen or not, I love the ending,' said Lily, 'He walks into Armani's and he's looking at jackets and a salesgirl comes up to him and says, "Can I help you, sir?" What a marvellous last line.'

They agreed it was a marvellous ending, one that only a writer of fiction could have dreamed up.

~

It was the Ashwins who sent a glittery invitation with an accompanying note on creamy monogrammed paper from Arati. They had heard. They were so sorry. She must come. Rehana decided to accept because it was time to be out and about. She dressed with a touch of frivolity for her return to the world in chiffon, gold bangles, gold sandals, and eye shadow.

Scotch was being served in squat square crystal glasses—a shape it was hard to get her hand around—in the velvet-curtained Persian-carpeted drawing room of the Ashwins' penthouse suite in their hotel. Champagne went by in crystal flutes, kababs and caviar on silver salvers. Arati Ashwin looked ravishing with Lily's creation billowing airily over her baby bump and around her girth. Lily was a genius. Rehana had expected the evening to have a formal tread about it, but ambassadors, movie stars, news anchors and other leading lights were standing around at their chatty intimate ease as if what the invitation had called a resurrection of national culture happened every day. It looked like a cozy family get-together. She stood at the edge of the party, clutching her square glass, hearing a man say killing the lover made it a 'crime passionel', not a crime.

Arati spotted her and led her into the gathering. 'You must meet Andy. His company has done the public relations for our event to put it on the map worldwide.'

Andy had the glow and affability of professional accomplishment. He and Nalin had been at Princeton together and this had been a most original assignment, spreading the word about a Hindu kingdom.

'Kingdom?'

'A slip of the tongue. That's what Nepal used to be. There are Christian, Buddhist and Muslim nations. Why not a Hindu one? The time is good and ripe for it. Definition is what it's about around the world. We specialize in policy makeovers.'

In answer to why it needed to be known worldwide, he replied, laughing, 'You don't exist if nobody knows you exist, and that's not as crazy as it sounds. Events have to get heard about. And PR gets practical results.'

Long before his time the company had done a job to boost Pinochet in Chile after his coup got rid of Allende. The results were there for all to see. Foreign capital rolled in, the economy boomed and there wasn't a thing you could buy in New York or Paris that you couldn't buy in Chile. Andy was twiddling the ice cubes in his Scotch on the rocks with one finger. She swallowed some of hers for its chloroforming effect, putting away the faceless bodies, scattered tongues and eyeballs of the disappeared in Pinochet's Chile.

'The company has done makeovers for celebrities too. President Carter's ratings went up when we got him to stop smiling. It made him look weak and undecided.'

In his polite American way Andy asked her what she did and Rehana explained. He looked politely sympathetic as over the death of a distant aunt for whom burial was the answer. It was his opinion there was no way around that problem. Not much could be done about it. Torture was here to stay like the arms race where it had to be weapon for weapon if you wanted to stay ahead. Power depended on it, on staying ahead of the competition whatever it took.

Arati took Andy away and Rehana went toward the beckoning arm near the bar across the room. Gaurav, dean of art critics, greeted her glumly, exchanging his empty glass for a full one.

'What's the matter, Gaurav?'

'The guidelines, what else? No breasts, no buttocks, no pubic hair, no abstract art. The word is holy art, healthy art, national art.' He helped himself dejectedly from a bowl of caviar. They had been given a preview of the entries selected for culture week.

'This too shall pass is what you're hoping, Rehana? Maybe so. Art may survive but judging by elsewhere, critics don't.' He signalled a passing waiter. 'Meanwhile there's caviar. Have some.'

'Who's the European in a sari talking to Nalin Ashwin?'

'Where have you been, Rehana? She's a German expert on womb science. She's written a book about Germany's remarkable rise after the two World Wars being due to the racial purification they went in for and the perfect Aryan specimens they produced. The DCT has invited her here to set up clinics like they had in Germany to produce pure Aryan babies. Right colour, right height, right measurements. Our very own master race, Indian style. The shastras and shlokas come into it. The position of the planets decides when to fuck and when not to. A darn sight fancier than the Nazi no-nonsense technique. Now that racial cleansing is under way with outsiders being ghettoed, Aryanization is taking a great leap forward. No, I'm not drunk.'

A stranger was approaching, his face and height distinctly familiar as he drew nearer. Seeing she was trying to place him, he said, 'We met at Franz Rohners' book launch. We were eating camembert. My name is Zamir. I heard about the exhibition. I was planning to go to it.'

She nodded, the memory of it constricting her throat.

'I heard you were there.'

She nodded dumbly again.

'Hari said you might need a lift home. I can give you a lift when you're ready to leave.'

She cleared her throat and said she was ready.

Zamir drove at snail's pace. His car crawled and stalled through the dark along their traffic-bound side of the road. On the clear side cars raced unobstructed. A hard-hit object hurtled across the divide. The glare of passing headlights shone on and off a corpse. The corpse stirred. Zamir got out to investigate, ignoring the cacophony of horns behind him as traffic lights changed. He picked up the mongrel and Rehana reached back to open the passenger door for him to lay the mangled body on the seat.

'She's alive but barely,' he said, driving on.

'What are you going to do with her?'

'Take her home and see what I can do. I'll take her to a vet tomorrow if she survives. But I'll drop you home first. I have to go much further on.'

'No,' said Rehana on an impulse, 'I'll come with you. You'll need help.' Very reluctantly he agreed.

She had no watch on and no idea of the time as they left the main road and drove on. It could have been midnight when they arrived. The stars looked down on a soundless world where nothing breathed. Lights were on in his house, left on, he said, to discourage break-ins. His arms were cradling the bitch and she was asked to get his house key out of his pocket and open the door. She fumbled with the heavy lock, finally turning the key in it. Inside, she followed his laconic instructions, fetching newspaper to lay the body on, watching him tie the hind leg hanging loose to a makeshift splint, handing him wet cloths soaked in antiseptic to clean and disinfect gashes in the dirty blood-matted hair, and finally a mug of water with a teaspoon to slide drops of it into the side of the mouth. Getting to his feet Zamir announced, 'That's all we can do'—the longest sentence spoken since they had entered the house—and went to the bathroom to wash his hands. Rehana stood holding the empty mug. She was gripped by a sense of powerlessness over things she could do nothing about. The mug slipped from her nerveless fingers and hit the floor with a clatter. Pain stung her jaw on its assaulted side. Knives glinted, flashing past. Iron split wood. Glass crashed and splintered under pounding feet. Sharp slivers of it raked her skin. Her legs gave way. She dropped into the chair behind her, hunched over and wept hysterically into her lap. When her frenzy wore down she sat up dazed and dishevelled. The room around her took blurred shape, slow to clear. It was calm, quiet, unravaged. A rolled carpet stood upended in a corner. Pictures waiting for walls lay stacked on bare floor alongside cloth piles folded wrong side out that must be curtains waiting to be hung. She drank the glass of water Zamir brought. He pulled her to her feet, leaned her briefly against him to steady her and said, 'Let's go.'

She found her gold mesh purse under her chair and followed him out. In the car she was assailed by smells of Dettol, Lifebuoy and wounded animal that clung to his clothes. At some stage of the drive home she recovered her tongue and was able to ask him why he had chosen to live at such a distance.

'I didn't choose. My landlord demanded my apartment back. He said the other tenants wanted me out and it was best for my safety as well as his own. No one would rent me another. Finally I had to move a long way out.'

She had a nagging need to ask him something important and kept trying to remember what it was. Giving up, she asked if they could meet one day soon. Zamir said he would be in touch.

Franz wrote back in answer to her last mail, sounding elated about culture week and the paintings selected for it. From the point of view of his researches, it was bracing news. It fitted perfectly into his study of revolutions. Had he not said they repeat each other ad infinitum, imitate and echo each other? She must let him know if this culture week would also have a parade because the Third Reich's culture had been launched with a five-mile parade. A procession of knights in armour, Valkyries and Rhine maidens was followed by the Wehrmacht marching in magnificent precision. The soldiers of the SS brought up the rear in the famous black uniforms of their awesome corps. Franz had a diary in his possession describing it. The diarist, Erich, had been there on that July afternoon in 1939. A day of national pride, Erich had noted. Munich was gaily decorated and the whole city had turned out to watch the parade. The Fuhrer himself was there watching it for the entire two and a half hours. For Erich it had been a thrilling emotional experience.

'What you say of your stormtroopers' fury,' wrote Franz, 'how familiar that, too, is. Like at the Batlivala gallery, all the masterpieces of modern art were cleared out of German museums and healthy art was hung in the new House of German Art: peasants ploughing German soil, happy German families, heroes of Greek mythology dressed up like Hitler Youth in brown shorts and black belts. But unlike your guidelines there were nudes, male and female anatomies of the purest Aryan proportions. It is said the Fuhrer stood admiring the Swan raping Leda and bought it for his own collection. In case you don't know this Greek myth, Rehana, it is Zeus disguised as a swan who rapes Leda. But the painting that rejoiced the Fuhrer had a Wagnerian Swan about to rape a German maiden.'

Franz was relieved to know her face had mended except for the barest scars, her eye could open wide and her other wounds had healed. As for the destruction of Nikhil's and all the modern masterpieces, the deepest mourning would not be deep enough. As in nature, it is the prelude. First the skies darken, then comes the storm. Trees know it is coming when their leaves start to shiver.

'In times like these, Rehana, marvels like duck l'orange, the spy sagas of Le Carre, and *C'est si Bon* on the immortal Satchmo's trumpet, are gifts sent to us to assuage our grief.'

To these gifts Rehana could have added 'the

glimmer of moonbeams through iron grating for the prisoner on her jail cot.'

The post brought contracts from Franz for her to sign and return. He had found a publisher for two of her father's books.

~

The telephone beside his bed rang. Kamlesh picked it up on the first ring. Calls at unearthly hours of the night were Gayatri's, this time not for one of her work-related chats or nuggets of news passed on for his interest or enjoyment. She sounded urgent. She was upset and alarmed by the news. Was it true? Why was his book being junked? Was he in trouble? Should she consult a lawyer about it? The last question was a quintessentially Gayatri reaction.

'What in heaven's name would a lawyer in Peru know about censorship in India?' he said in late-night exasperation.

'Let me tell you, Kris,'—an abbreviation she had coined that had no connection with his name—'there is nothing this continent doesn't know about censorship, crackdowns, invasions, coups and assassinations. This continent has been through it all. How else could they have produced such amazing writers?'

Gayatri's immersion into the past and present of wherever she was posted was legendary. It made her brilliant at her work.

'So, what's happening about your book, Kris?'

'All I know is someone on an investigating committee rang my publisher and asked him questions about me. Sudhir is going to tell me about it at lunch tomorrow.'

'Then I'll ring again tomorrow night.'

Universal Books specialized in history and politics. Sudhir had had a healthy respect for Kamlesh since they had published his *Genie* two years ago. The title notwithstanding, and in Sudhir's opinion its starry-eyed view of the Non-

Aligned Movement, the book had apparently brought recent history alive for its inheritors. Sales had been consistently high. Their association had ripened into a warmth beyond business matters.

'They don't want it said they are banning books, so they are just disappearing them,' he told Kamlesh when they were seated at his Kashmir Club, 'like inconvenient people were disappeared in Chile and Argentina and other places and only their bones were left to tell the tale. But as books have no bones there's nothing left to prove they were there. Anyway, don't let that spoil our lunch.'

Sudhir, a strict non-vegetarian, proceeded to order kabargah, dum kaleji and shaljam salan with rumali rotis, and a bit of vegetable on the side.

'The man who came to see me wanted to know your political affiliations.'

'I don't have any,' said Kamlesh.

'He says your praise of non-alignment shows your political affiliations.'

'It's ridiculous. The book is about the end of empires, the birth of nations, and a huge change in how the world was run.'

Sudhir had brought a copy of *Genie* with him. He handed it to Kamlesh across the table. 'I've highlighted the parts that are causing trouble.'

Kamlesh flipped through it and came to a highlighted passage. He read it aloud: 'Hardly had one war ended when another had begun with wartime's victorious allies now sworn enemies divided by an arms race against each other. Better had the atom not been split, and the power to annihilate millions with a single bomb never been placed in human hands.'

'And further on you are weeping for the Japanese people,' said Sudhir.

'People don't want wars. They don't make wars. They only get killed in them. And the atom bomb was not the end of the story. After the war they tested their H-bomb on Bikini, never mind the people who lived on the island. There was never a greater need for non-alignment. I've said so.'

'I know. It makes you out to be a pacifist,' said Sudhir playing devil's advocate, 'and that's not allowed nowadays.'

'It was never allowed. Anti-war campaigners are dangerous bloody nuisances. Locking them up has always been policy. But I'm not a pacifist.'

'I believe you, but these investigators ferret out what suits them and make what they like out of it. They are saying you were against the Vietnam war when you were a student and you marched in an anti-war procession.'

'Of course I did. I happened to be in Calcutta and I joined in and shouted "amar nam, tomar nam, Vietnam" with all the rest.'

Sudhir enjoyed that recollection. A meal that had looked enormous to Kamlesh was, to his surprise, getting steadily eaten while they talked. Outrage stimulated appetite.

'As you say, Kamlesh, being anti-war has always been dangerous. But now, my friend, it's blasphemous. Your investigator says war has the sanction of our scripture. It's the plot of our sacred books. It's what they are about. Opposing war makes you sacrilegious along with the fact that your book is a security risk now when we are threatened. I forgot to ask him by whom.'

Over steaming fragrant kahwa Sudhir warned, 'The man may call on you. I am more sorry than I can say about the book, Kamlesh. Apart from anything else, it means big returns gone down the drain. We could have fought for it on any other ground but charges of blasphemy and national security make it impossible.'

'It's a good thing I don't have to earn my living by writing,' said Kamlesh.

He repeated the conversation to Gayatri when she rang that night.

'What you make a living by is the next thing they will go after,' she warned. 'That's the well-known sequence.'

'In the Peruvian lawyer's opinion no doubt. But we're not Peru, Gayatri. For God's sake, we've grown up in freedom. This is India.'

Queer how those three words had a liberating effect.

'You know, Kris, you've had your head buried in Shah Jahan's incest and his other shenanigans. You haven't noticed what's going on around you or believed it's for real. Please keep in mind what my Peruvian friend says. I tell you these people have known all about such matters since their Incan empire.'

Gayatri's opinions came of her own colourful reasoning. Regardless of the Peruvian lawyer and Peru's tormented history Kamlesh fell sound asleep.

In his office a few days later he got up and stood at the window. It was what he often did when composing reports, stare out of the window until words came. This afternoon none came. His mind revolted at the thought of submitting to the death of his career. No investigator had come to see him as Sudhir had warned, only a letter informing him he had two choices. He could resign from the service with immediate effect or be summoned for an official enquiry. In other times sacrilege had faced an Inquisition that burned heretics at the stake. The charges against him would 'detain' him behind bars for no known length of time. The country had to be protected from the danger of peace.

His father had joined the foreign service at its creation after independence and Kamlesh had grown up on talk of beginnings. A new nation, flag, anthem. A republic proclaimed, its foundations laid on ideas that became the nation's meaning. There had been the grouses and grumbles of a newborn service that was poor and powerless, unversed in power-play, and up against hoary wielders of power, yet had made its voice heard in its own vocabulary: West Asia instead of Middle East, Asian, not Asiatic, Muslim, not

Moslem, and other more significant corrections to the skewed perceptions set down in history as indisputable. It had taken stamina and sly humour to insist on being oneself. When an irate Dulles barked, 'Once and for all, are you with us or against us?' Nehru replied, 'Yes.' When a roomful of power-wielders demanded, 'What is your country doing about population control?' they were told about the woman seeking foolproof contraception and her doctor prescribing a glass of water. 'Is that all, doctor? Before or after?' and the doctor saying, 'Instead, Madam, instead.' Laughter brim-filling the room. What other way was there to remind the powerful, the prosperous, the arrived, what they had forgotten about the pains of arrival?

They tell us there's nothing new under the sun but that's not true, Kamlesh's father had said, we trod new ground. We blazed a trail: no taking sides with warring Powers, no joining their wars, no giving them bases to bomb others from, no truck with war. It's peace we're after. Now, thought Kamlesh, we're in the race for bigger, better, deadlier. His inquisitors were right about his book. The pursuit of peace violated holy writ.

The letter of resignation he knew he must write came to him, page after page of strongly worded, reasoned, seasoned argument. He went back to his desk, sat down and rubbished it all. Explanations were for prisoners in the dock. His anger dictated one precise sentence. He wrote it with a Parker pen in thick black ink on official stationery, had it delivered, and sat on at his desk. His palms felt clammy on its familiar ink-stained surface, his fingers traced its dents and scars. His closed eyes summoned the angles and corners of the room he knew by heart. The best of his knowledge, experience and ideals had found expression at this desk, in this room. It was not the last time he would be in it. He would have to come again to clear up, but never again would he be here as of right. He had not imagined that losing the work he had given his life to would be so devastating. Regret, heartbreak, desolation welled up in him.

At home he immersed himself in Shah Jahan, concentrating on completing a book that might not see the light. Sudhir had cautioned it would be wise to wait until the furore died down and his name got crossed off the inquisitors' Most Wanted list. These things blow over. Now that he had resigned, he would be forgotten. Be that as it may, a book once begun and long lived with could not be left unfinished. Kamlesh got on with it. The Taj love story had had the most dismal of endings, with the lover who built it dying ill, old and wretched, imprisoned in the Akbarabad fort. Kamlesh decided on a livelier ending for his book. He found the grande finale he needed in a contemporary account of Jahanara's extravagant grief for her father/lover describing her as 'The precious pearl of the casket of chastity, (who with) the other respected ones of the holy precincts of fortune and honour, turned their rose-coloured faces into blue-hued ones through blows and slaps of grief, shedding oceans and oceans of lustrous pearls on the earth from the oysters of their eyes...'

Gayatri rang to say her assignment in Peru had come to an end and she would be coming back soon. No news or ministry gossip had reached her about where she was likely to be posted next. She would stay with her sister till she found a place of her own.

The Taj story completed and put away, Kamlesh was able to come out of his book-imposed cloister and ask Gayatri's sister for news of her arrival. He made a note of the date, airline, flight and time and told Malti he would meet Gayatri at the airport and drop her off, it would be no trouble. Malti gratefully accepted his offer. She dreaded having to cope with parking, luggage, flight delays and other airport miseries.

The plane was on time. Gayatri came out of

the terminal, caught sight of Kamlesh and stayed rooted where she was, unrecognizably mute and stricken. Something was inconceivably wrong. Illness, disaster, worse. Ice touched the pit of his stomach. Grim possibilities closed in on him. Fear propelled him forward. Gayatri flung her arms around him and clung to him crying 'Oh Kris, what have they done to you?' Hardly daring to breathe his arms tightened fiercely around the long-lost cherished feel of her. It did not seem possible they had ever been parted.

'Where to?' he asked, starting the car.

Still shaken but with a ghost of her sparkle, she said, 'Home, of course, Kris. I'll ring Malti from home.'

Malti received the news of their change in living arrangements with outer matter-of-factness and vast inner relief. She had almost given up hope of their seeing the light.

~

Cocktails at the Nirvana bar had been long postponed but at last a date could be agreed upon and they were there, Gayatri with them. The bar was seductively low-lit and designed for intimacy. A waiter stood nearby, looking past them.

'Funny how he doesn't see five of us,' said Lily. 'D'you suppose he's waiting for the men of the party to arrive?'

She lifted an arm for his attention, which he saw and raised his own hand as if to say he'd seen.

'I'll have to go and collar him,' said Lily, when they saw a man crossing the room, coming towards their table. He and Gayatri greeted each other with delight, kissing each other on both cheeks after which she introduced her friend, Carlos, the Cuban ambassador. The ambassador sketched a salute in graceful acknowledgement of their smiles and took in the four new faces with evident admiration. It was a far cry from the meaningless gallantries that social graces seemed to require and which they despised. The ambassador was clearly a man to be cultivated.

'Join us, do,' urged Lily, backed by her companions.

Alas, he had to decline as he was just leaving. Some friends from home were coming to dinner to celebrate Fidel's survival of the CIA's forty-fifth attempt to assassinate him.

'They never give up, do they?' said Gayatri.

Their own delayed tribute to Lily's enhanced income owing to the new Nazi policy of permanent pregnancy seemed unworthy in comparison. Instead of joining them which he would have been happy to do, Carlos asked their permission to order a celebratory Cuban cocktail for them to toast Fidel. The waiter came with full speed. Daiquiris were ordered and paid for and Carlos said a heartfelt goodbye. He would have stayed but for Fidel's and his country's continuing good fortune.

They toasted Fidel in all solemnity but the

heady Cuban cocktail and the reason for it had a sobering effect. Fresh from South America, Gayatri said, 'These things happen to them all the time. They're geared for the worst. We go on saying it can't happen here. Being India will protect us, as Kris kept thinking, even when the signs were clear as day. Fancy Kris, an experienced observer like him, not realizing what was coming to him.'

Rehana sensed an unspoken belated agreement amongst Gayatri's four listeners that they had been wrong and fiction had got it right. Kamlesh, like the manor in Rehana's book choice, had not noticed the centipedal slither of things to come. A reminder that but for art, we would never know the truth.

The waiter came to remove their empty glasses and place five more daiquiris before them.

'We didn't order more,' protested Lily, and was informed that the gentleman had placed a double order.

'Well, to Fidel again and Cuba,' said Gayatri, picking up her glass and clinking theirs.

~

Gangu was off duty and Rehana was in the kitchen cooking. Kamlesh's description of his meaty lunch with his publisher had put her in mind of her Nani's incomparable koftas. Abdul watched her fingers blend oil and curd, masalas and hingh into the mince. He was standing by ready to chop and slice as he did to help Gangu and was looking on in fascination. No onion, no garlic, then how meat?

Rehana introduced him to the secret of hingh. He watched her make sausage shapes of the mince in the palm of one hand and deliver them delicately to ghee and curd in the frying pan. He was an eager learner, taking the pan from Rehana and moving the koftas around with care. He asked if he could use one of the suitcases that had held her father's books for his own belongings and give the other one to his friend Suraj who worked in his father's shop of kitchen utensils in the market. Suraj could come and collect it after eight o'clock when his father closed the shop. Rehana knew Dhiru's shop, invitingly stocked with stainless steel and shining brass.

She worked late after dinner finishing a report for the group with her favourite ghazals as background music to keep out traffic and night noises, but all was peace and stillness when the music stopped and her work was done. She walked out into a moonlit brilliance that had the caressing mildness of late spring, the gentle interlude between winter and the harsh heat to come. The garden slept. Its fragrances floated up to receive her gratitude. She strolled out to the far end of the lane where the old flowerpot vendor lived under his tarpaulin shelter and stored his gamlas, displaying them on the main road for buyers when morning came. He was awake, sitting huddled and half hidden. On the ground opposite him the shock of a human mound held her rigid. At sight of her the old man gabbled, beseeching help. Eight of them came, she kept hearing, would come back if they had seen him, if they knew he had seen four of them tear the clothes off the boy, force him to his knees, swing their rods high and then down to break his back and crack his skull, shouting what leather is this, is this suitcase made of cowhide as if the dead can answer. Bright moonlight burnished the skin torn off the blood-reddened back. Greyish slime oozed from the split skull. Rehana had heard him and Abdul clowning in the kitchen while she was having her dinner.

Everything in her ground to a halt yet her brain worked, informing her this was no clumsy haphazard killing. Four had surrounded him. What of the other four? They had watched, memorizing which blows where and how many. The mathematics of it had been tried, practised and perfected somewhere else, and somewhere else before that. The act of killing had been fined down to a repeatable reliable recipe. It did what a single bullet or a spray of bullets could not do. Alive one minute, dead the next, was not the purpose. It was the interval in between that punished.

Rehana found herself on her knees beside the body, as paralyzed as he had been, confronted by deadly danger. She felt the terror of being encircled by weapons poised to strike, the helplessness of skin and spine against the savagery to come. Feeling went no further. In the unbridgeable chasm between herself and the sufferer, between one person and another, her flesh could not feel, nor ever know the agony his flesh had endured. She willed herself upright, straightened her buckling knees and walked back to do what had to be done. Suraj's body, Suraj's father, the police. At some hour of what remained of the night she said a requiem for the faith of her fathers. Sanatan dharma had been slaughtered in cold blood this night.

The group took charge. She would not have known what to do. She didn't know hierarchy had the last word in death as in life. An empty field outside city limits had to be found for the cremation, the sticks and twigs and fallen branches collected by them augmented by logs purloined from a place they knew, a makeshift platform awkwardly constructed. No priest, no prayer, only themselves and Dhiru, made of stone, beside them. Stone cannot light a fire. Someone had to. She took the lighted stick handed to her and did as she was told, stepping back as the wood kindled and a wisp of smoke began its spiral into the darkening sky.

The next day they found the utensils shop had been ransacked. It was expected, the group told her, for selling kitchenware that caste Hindus would cook their food in and eat out of, a man ordained to skin dead cattle, lift roadside garbage and high-caste shit, pretending to be what he wasn't and thinking he could get away with it. Ungrateful, these chamaars, though they were allowed to sell the skin and bones and other body parts of the carcasses they skinned. Dhiru had disappeared.

The police reported a body found mysteriously dead.

~

Zamir arrived unexpectedly. In the effort of carrying on Rehana had forgotten she had asked him to come. He said he had taken a chance and dropped in without warning as he found he had a free morning. Free from what? She knew nothing about him. He was a stranger she had met twice before. Conversation had hardly figured in their acquaintance, and their last meeting had ended in her uncontrollable breakdown. She now remembered why she had asked to meet him again. It was where he lived, at a safe distance from the eyes and ears of the city's centre. That, and something to do with his personality, the deliberate way he had gone about rescuing the mongrel, ignoring the cacophony of car horns behind him and getting on with what had to be done. The poor creature had died, he told her. She must have been past saving when he rescued her.

The lawn was damp from watering. They stood on the verandah, she wondering how to ask a favour of him when he went down the steps to the wet grass to look at Abdul's flowerbeds, and then in comic bewilderment at her, making her smile. After a puzzled second—making sure she actually knew how to?—he smiled warmly back, came up the steps and sat down. The reason for his visit was slipping from her. She called it back, remembering why she had wanted to meet him again. It was where he lived, at a safe distance from here, and the need to find work and shelter for Hanif, the boy Cyrus had rescued from the ghetto, and his mother. She explained the vital reason for it. Would it be possible for them to work and live somewhere out there? Zamir thought about it. For a tailor there was sure to be work. About Hanif he was less certain until Abdul came out with guava juice and Zamir was reminded he had not yet found household help. If Hanif would work for him, Zamir would make sure he had time to paint. This unexpected solution and the enormous relief of it took Rehana unawares. When she collected herself and thanked him it was with an intensity that made him ask if she was responsible for their safety.

'No. Yes,' she replied, not bothering to elaborate.

It was a long time since she had felt so much herself in a masculine presence and exactly like this never before, a feeling she did not put down entirely to his having seen her break down for no apparent reason that night, but rather because he hadn't asked her why. It was a habit he apparently had of ignoring what came in the way of getting on with what had to be done which dispensed with the need for explanation. However, one does not sit saying nothing when one's guest is occupying the other chair on the verandah and conversation is supposed to be made which was what she was not doing.

A brief peaceful silence later he said, 'I would have come sooner but I had visitors.'

His doorbell had rung. He had answered it. Men walked in. One sat down, the others stood. They were deputed to collect books for neighbourhood book-burning fiestas. His was on their list. They had come for it. The standing men parted to let him through. He brought his copies and handed them over. Rehana's immediate shock came of hearing he had written a book.

His latest novel, he said, *Unholy Love*. Rehana sat up, her shock complete. The stark unfolding of the tale and her admiration for it was as vivid as the day she had read it but the despair of a lifetime spent removing filth was by someone else. She heard Zamir say it was his pseudonym, no longer a protection. She was appalled. Could he be serious? Huge ancient megaliths and mountainsides had not withstood religious wrath, what hope was there for a pseudonym? The week-ago night returned, the murder of Suraj securely welded to crimes past and to come. What crimes? Bodies had been found mysteriously dead. She asked Zamir what he was going to do. The men had told him this was a warning. He was sitting with his long legs stretched out, his hands resting on the arms of the garden chair, his eyes on the flurry of a flight of sparrows from a low-hanging branch of the cassia.

His novel, a horror story made luminous in the telling had affected and enchanted her as nothing had in recent literature. But knowing a novel was not knowing the writer, there seldom being a congruence between the two. She waited for what she knew he was going to say, 'I must get out, go away somewhere so that I can write in safety.' He turned to look at her and said instead, 'I must get started on a new novel' and then, 'Can I take you out to lunch?'

They lunched at home, the longest lunch in recent times. Rehana talked of what was uppermost in her mind, his novel and its unbelievable happy ending. Zamir agreed with her emphatically. It was a most unlikely ending and not one he had written. The character had chosen it. Set characters down on a page and they take over, as when dance takes over the dancer, and song the singer, or when a swimmer high-dives in an arc of its own volition and not the swimmer's. Or when a woodcutter's axe becomes a rhythm that takes over. The illustrations were endless, he said. Rehana listened, attracted by his workmanlike illustrations. She understood what he was saying, but would anyone ever understand the mystery, the sorcery, of that transforming moment? Talk extended over coffee and after, shared talk about shared passions.

That night she woke with a start and reached for her bedside lamp. His arm was there before hers, switching it on. The moon outside her window was seven days thinner, waning ritually, indifferently as if it had not lit up an orgy of blood and brain seven days ago. She turned and wound her arms around Zamir in a strangling grip, pushing her face against his chest for deliverance from the sight, repeating, 'I can't go on with it, I won't go on with it.' It was a decision she made from time to time.

Next afternoon she was at the site with her group, looking down, forcing her gaze downward on naked buttocks branded with a swastika. Another body branded Om across torn breasts, stared up at her. A pregnant belly had been sliced open, the pulp that had been a foetus plucked out and tossed aside. Legs lay wrenched apart, metal rods inserted. Smoke was rising from the smouldering flesh of a neatly constructed human pyramid. Rehana stood soldered to the ground. The ghetto Hanif had escaped had crumbled. Fires raged among the ruins. Her companions were picking their way through bodies intertwined in death by arms, legs and heads flung over each other, looking for a sign or a flicker of life. The group's founder was making a tour, counting corpses, two hundred and fifty female and as many or more butchered males. He was speaking to the policemen on duty, asking how. Who knows but it is said an explosion caused by a leaking cylinder had set the tenement on fire, Rehana heard a policeman say. So careless, these people. We have been sent for to collect the bodies for burial. There will be no delay, the graves are ready, dug deep for mass burial. She recalled Cyrus telling her the DCT was in charge of racial purity and the ghetto came under his watch.

At the DCT's office they were cordially received and invited to sit in a semi-circle in front of the shining expanse of his desk. The purpose of their visit? Ah yes, the fire. He listened gravely, saying he was aware of the unfortunate incident, he had received a full report, and he understood their concern. But however regretful, this is not a matter for your group, my friends, an accidental fire caused by carelessness as so often happens.

Rehana sat forward in her chair, speaking succinctly for the group, stating it was torture they had come about, the butchery, the branding, the mutilation. Well aware that the words had grown sterile with repetition and no longer shocked whoever heard or read them, she had made it a practice to describe the result in each such case in precise detail. A solemn silence from the DCT who inclined his head, waiting for more, his hands clasped loosely on his desk. Well then she would give him more. She had no proof, only her profound inner conviction backed by knowledge gained from Franz, for what she said next. It was a case of arson, she declared. It was one of the uniformed tribe who had set fire to the building. The tribe itself had come armed with Stone Age and newer weapons, prepared to massacre. The mass graves dug beforehand to speed disposal gave her announcement absolute authority.

The DCT's face cleared as though all was now understood. His hands unclasped and spread wide in appeal. If what you say is true, my friends, even should that be the case, then is it not natural? Should our people not get carried away remembering our history? Is it not reasonable that they should do to our tormentors what our tormentors did to us? And now, my friends, let me offer you my cardamom tea. Its fragrance is unrivalled among teas.

~

One day a wild wind blew through life on earth, wrote Franz to Rehana with his typical flourish. You have seen what wild winds do, whip branches bare of flower and foliage, and so with those that sweep nations, as this extract from Erich's journal shows. I am sending it to you for a reason I will come to after you have read it. But first, here is what Erich writes in his journal:

There comes a point in life when there is no turning back. For me it came as I watched the parade in Munich that July day of 1939. It was a parade of our culture, from the classical to the present time when we are a military Power like none other ever before and the magnificent marching figures of the Wehrmacht and the SS displayed our military might. The SS soldiers were unique. The insignia on their black uniforms looked like strokes of lightning above daggers and death's head badges, a uniform that sets them apart as the Party's own soldiers, to deal with its enemies. But they are also chosen for their racial purity. Herr Himmler who is Reichsfuhrer of the SS in charge of national security and racial purity is known to oversee the selection process himself which screens candidates for the weight, height, and bodily proportions by which an Aryan is known, and it is Herr Himmler who set up the training years ago that hardens their minds and prepares them for the tasks they have been chosen to perform. I knew as I watched the procession go past that it was the career for me. I had the Nordic features, the hair colour, eye colour and physique for it. That day it became my ambition to serve in the SS.

How am I to put into words my excitement at being selected and to learn we are handpicked to carry out the national policy of increasing the numbers of the racially pure. The Fuhrer's slogan 'Europe today, tomorrow the world!' forsees a future ruled by a master race of surpassing fitness. Survival of the fittest is common knowledge—the Fuhrer has called it 'the iron law of nature'—yet who but he has had the genius to apply this law of nature to the human species of the white race to evolve what Nietzsche called Ubermensch, a superman who will be as superior to ordinary mortals as men are to apes. This dream we are called upon to serve is the religion of the Third Reich.

Clinics have been set up for Lebensborn, this 'fountain of life' experiment that is new to humankind. There we bring blue-eyed blonde German women—golden blonde, butter blonde, silver blonde—and mate with them. Women are also brought from Norway that is now occupied by us. We do our part. It is an act to be efficiently performed, ramming through resistance to achieve results. There is no question of sexual pleasure given or taken, though there is no lack of sexual pleasure in our lives. Thrilled by our victories in war, enthralled by our uniform, inspired by the spirit of the times, women go with us for the asking. The Lebensborn clinics are for the science of eugenics. The body under you

enclosing your member is there for penetration
and impregnation. The larger programme for
racial purification and racial hygiene sterilizes
or exterminates sub-humans. These are the
Jews and the weak and useless people among
us as well as those in the countries we have
occupied.

That is what this diarist writes but he does not
say what became of the pregnant women or the
children born of the Third Reich's religious fervour.
The women gave birth in secret in Lebensborn
homes and were sent back to wherever they came
from. Their racially pure offspring were put into
special orphanages or given to Nazi couples to
bring up, and were christened in a sacred ritual
with an SS dagger held over the infant while the
foster mother swore to uphold the Nazi ideology.
Those that were born disabled or defective, or later
became so, were killed or sent for extermination
to concentration camps.

Can this be true, how can it be, you must be asking as you read this, Rehana. It is a question we keep asking and others after us will keep asking though it was all revealed at the Nuremberg trials. There are realities that imagination cannot conceive of and will not allow, making us cling to how can it be.

So this is the family matter I told you I was writing about because I myself and Gerda were conceived in Lebensborn clinics by unknown Erichs of the SS. Our unknown mothers gave birth in one of the twenty Lebensborn homes in Germany and Norway. At our christenings under SS daggers our foster mothers swore allegiance to the Nazi religion, and we would have grown up to become the next generation of the master race if in our infancy the war had not cut short the next thousand years of the Reich. Instead we grew up, myself here and Gerda in Norway, reviled, abused and hated as offspring of Nazi eugenics, to discover each other years later. This was at a meeting of other Lebensborn offspring trying to find some comfort in each other in our shameful common predicament. Imagine that you are looking into a mirror, only it is not a mirror but another person in a roomful of other persons who like mirrors are reflecting and repeating you. No, it was not quite like that, it never could be exactly that, but the attempt had thrown up likenesses, those unlike having been eliminated at the start.

Thank God, you will say, that what I have been calling revolutions or transformations or by whatever name they choose to call themselves do not all go so far. Yet they do, if not to manufacture racially pure anatomies then to manufacture minds that mirror each other's so that you do not know your thought from another's because they are the same thought. Why else the purges and massacres if not to purge us of the danger of thinking differently? Think like me or face extermination. On and on they will go, Rehana, until exterminators realize we are born to be different from one another, nature has made us so. I once saw a carpet I was told was handmade true Persian which is what I wanted as a gift for Gerda. On careful examination I found its design was exactly similar along all its borders and all through its entire length and breadth as only a machine-made product can be. In handcrafting there will be at least a shadow of a fault, which is the mark of a human hand and its claim to authenticity. But we will talk of all this when we meet soon because Gerda and I have accepted the invitation of Nalin Ashwin to come for the culture week and we shall be there for the grand opening. Speaking as a writer, it will give me the ending for my new book on my family matter, though it gives me no pleasure that the disastrous link between you and us is now established beyond doubt and the past of my country has become the future of yours. Have I not said all revolutions, transformations, or call them what you may, follow the trodden path?

~

Rehana wondered at the most remarkable days of her life going by unremarked, already a habit. Zamir, helped by Hanif and Hanif's mother, unrolled carpets, hung curtains, placed furniture, books and possessions where day by day they would acquire the permanence they had lost in transit. A city's breadth away she carried out the jobs she was assigned in the campaign against torture and its cult of human sacrifice, covering her face with her hands against unbearable recurring images. There was no interruption in either life, both prizing the continuity essential for work. The wind blowing across the nation was left to blow while they grounded themselves afresh in their occupations, his to write, hers to act on behalf of. The time they spent apart was a renewal of resolve, time together a land of discovery. They were lovers who knew what lovers know, that no love is carved in the image of other loves. It is itself, forsaking all others. Fortune had favoured them by accident or chance. Neither of them believed in fate, so their meeting being destined was out of the question, leaving each of them secretly wondering what else it could be.

The question arose whether Rehana should accept the DCT's invitation to the gala opening of culture week. He was evidently still mindful of her drubbing and making up for it. Admit two, the invitation said, unnecessarily since Zamir baulked at missing precious hours of a whole morning's work. But Franz's impending arrival decided her and persuaded Zamir. Franz was looking forward to winding up his book with this climactic event on the path to cultural transformation. It would mark the announcement of Hindu nationhood, the Anno Domini from whence the new era would date, all else relegated to BCT. As always, it was following the well-established pattern. Our past is your future, he had written to Rehana.

~

The early summer day already felt hot on bare arms but the opening ceremony was to be under a shamiana on the spacious gracious lawn of the Directorate of Cultural Transformation's glass and steel high-rise. It was not yet the blistering heat that would wither the panorama of rose-red flowerbeds and the blush-pink beauties draping the garden wall. Astrologers had picked the day for its auspiciousness, but it could well have been picked with an eye for the lawn's lush greenness and the fragrance of flowers in bloom that a hotter sun would extinguish. It was still the season though fast approaching its end, for silk saris and kameezes adorned with a fashionable abundance of costume jewellery, dangling earrings, wristloads of bracelets, beringed fingers and the spangle and jangle of beads. The occasion demanded high fashion and cameras were poised for it as the shamiana filled with invited guests who had no premonition of, or preparation for the cow carcass on the rambler roses, its fore- and hind legs splayed rigidly on either side of the garden wall. An evil-smelling carcass landed near the shamiana, screams came from the shamiana as another descended on a flowerbed, burying it under the stench and fumes of putrefaction. A slight breeze lifted and wafted the fumes above and around. Under the canopy Rehana held down blowing strands of her contaminated hair and wiped her watering eyes. The lawn, a battlefield of stinking sunlit corpses in grotesque postures of rigor mortis, had no trees to obstruct the coming and going of their carriers. Rehana had the strange sensation of not believing what she was seeing, this declaration that Dalits would leave dead cows to rot: Here they are, all yours. Skin and chop them for disposal yourselves, it's not our job any more. Absurdly she looked for Dhiru in the tumult. Had he joined his outcaste comrades in their ultimatum to caste? How had they dared when lynch mobs roamed highways and byways in daylight and moonlight, skinning and slicing those they called cow thieves, cow traders, cow eaters, cow insulters?

The shamiana was a den of panic and suffocation, no way out of it. In its befouled smothering confinement a woman retched violently and vomited. Someone fainted.

Zamir pushed his way out, negotiating a track between carcasses, avoiding collision with rigid upright limbs or hind legs flung rigidly apart. Over the wall he saw corpse-filled trucks. Fifteen truckloads of decaying cows were taking time to offload. The road was in an uproar, shots being fired, police at war with truckers. No rules of warfare were being observed.

Rehana coughed and choked where she sat in a suffocating stupor, nauseous in the fumes. She reached for Zamir's hand, not there, his chair empty, no shoulder to lean on. She had an overwhelming desire to lean on his shoulder. She was aware of legs shuffling past, the shamiana slowly emptying, Zamir back and urging her to get up but first she had to tell him there was a sublime justice to it, this memorial of a kind to Suraj, the beauty and the poetry of this Dalit revolt. Zamir pulled her up as he had done that night and held her against him, this time in the passionate embrace of lovers in a perfumed paradise.

~

Three hours later at a table for six in the dining room of the Ashwin Hotel, menus lay unopened before them and napkins unfolded. The maitre d' hovered, muttering sotto voce. The city, the country, in shock—who could have foreseen and what now? He held his hand to his forehead as a Catholic would have made the sign of the cross and went away leaving them, he thought, to study their menus, but in reality to wonder at the morning. Left to themselves Franz admitted that his theory that all cultural transformations proceed along the same hallowed imitative path would have to be altered in his last paragraph. There were variations. Some proceed from below. It would seem we have here this exception. He would have to rewrite his ending. He looked around the table to encourage opinions.

Zamir said, 'As you see, endings have a way of writing themselves, as in novels.'

'Not so in politics,' Franz pointed out.

'Except at times when politics becomes poetry,' put in Kamlesh, 'as it has again and again,' and he gave examples. Gandhi. Rosa Parks. Mandela. Poetry had come from a prison cell in Nehru's words, 'Who lives if India dies? Who dies if India lives?' and at the stroke of a midnight to mark a tryst with destiny.

'But a novel has also given us darkness at noon,' said Franz. 'No poetry in that famous darkness. But yes, it seems there are exceptions.'

'Like this morning,' said Rehana.

The spectacle returned to astound them with its size and scale. Shackles had never been cast off at one blow. No ultimatum had been so astoundingly choreographed. The experienced researcher in Franz welcomed this dramatic unexpected conclusion to his manuscript, but for fear of subduing the rejoicing around the table he refrained from saying the end is not yet. In the days ahead there would be much work for Rehana and her group. He put on his glasses and picked up his menu, holding it open between him and Gerda. She put it firmly down.

Thought-reading is well-known to married couples. Gerda said reprovingly, 'All that may be so, Franz, but do you forget we are together to be joyful ? Where is the wine?'

The wine ordered, Franz picked up his menu again while the others, talking animatedly among themselves, seemed content to leave the choice of food to a connoisseur. This morning was proof to them the tide had turned, the monster of religious rule and holy war had been averted and all would be well. Franz did not know whether to weep or to marvel at such innocence in the face of all the evidence since time began. Instead he turned the pages of his menu to soups. Looking around the table he enquired, 'Shall we have vichyssoise to start with or,' turning another page, 'shall we start with shrimp?'

Acknowledgements

The extracts dated August 13, 1942 to August 22, 1942 from a prison diary are taken from the diary kept by my mother, Vijaya Lakshmi Pandit, during her third imprisonment, in Naini Central Jail, Allahabad during 1942-43. It was published by The Signet Press, Calcutta in 1946 under the title *Prison Days*.

The foreign travellers' views of Shah Jahan are taken from *Taj Mahal: The Illumined Tomb*, compiled by W.E. Begley and Z.A. Desai, published by The Aga Khan Program for Islamic Architecture, 1989.

Lightning Source UK Ltd.
Milton Keynes UK
UKHW04f0634260818
327814UK00011B/256/P

9 789386 702142